I0626685

This work is dedicated to…

the authors who live
within these pages, especially
William,
Charlotte,
Thomas,
George,
Emily,
Jane,
Alfred,
Branwell,
and
Anne.

Rest in Power.

Praise for The Netherfeld Trilogy

"Amber Elby crafts a world that invokes the best of Terry Pratchett, Ursula K. Le Guin, and Neil Gaiman, all rooted in the mythology of Shakespeare. The Netherfeld series is a must read for lovers of magic, the inexplicable, and especially the timeless wonder conjured by the plays of William Shakespeare."

~**Montgomery Sutton**, Shakespearean Actor, Director, and Playwright

"Reading Amber Elby's work is like walking down a pathway into my own childhood fairy land. All of the characters we love from Shakespeare come out to play, and we lose ourselves in her text as easily as one might get lost in the forest of Arden. Artists and readers will feel more seen with each turn of the page."

~**Victoria Rae Sook**, Artistic Director & Founder of *Food of Love* Productions

"Whip-smart, and I think would be just as much fun to read even if you had no knowledge of the Shakespeare characters it plays with— though if you do have this knowledge, you'll have some extra spice from seeing how Amber plays with it all… Five out of five cats!"

~**Asha & Tomte**, *A Cat, A Book, and A Cup of Tea Reviews*

"Like Shakespeare!? Like Percy Jackson? Imagine if you combine Rick Riordan's brilliance and Shakespeare's genius! What you get is the perfection that is Amber Elby's *Cauldron's Bubble* Series! All the adventure and heartbreak leaves you begging for more after each chapter. Well researched and thought out, and finally another non-toxic author! This series is what the world needs right now."

~**Alice D. Bloomer**, Actor & Producer of *Socially Distant Cymbeline*

"This series is almost impossible to put down. Elby truly captures Shakespeare's works with her adept writing… Similar to a puzzle, in my mind, that Elby pieces together beautifully."

~**Tiffany Salazar**, *Beyond the Stars Reviews*

"Not enough evil uncles in Narnia? Did Harry Potter leave you wishing for witches? Need more Banquos at the banquet in *Hunger Games*? Then enter the world of Netherfeld with Amber Elby's trilogy of Shakespeare-inspired adventures for lovers of fun and the fantastic. Step sideways into the universe of the Bard of Avon – you'll never see Shakespeare the same way again."

~**Jason Crane**, author of *Unexpected Sunlight* and the forthcoming *This Gorgeous Life*

Trouble Fires Burn

*A sorcerer's spell. A waning world.
And the wonder of Shakespeare.*

an original novel by
Amber Elby

Verdopolis Press

All rights reserved.
Copyright © 2021 by Amber Elby

Published by Verdopolis Press of Austin, Texas, United States of America.
ISBN- 978-1-7323142-5-2
Printed and bound in the United States of America.
First edition August 2019, revised edition August 2021.
Cover art by TypeJar Studio of Austin, Texas, United States of America.

No part of this book may be reproduced electronically,
mechanically, and/or by any other means, including recording
and/or photocopying, or adapted in any way without clear and
explicit written permission from the publisher or author.

Visit www.amberelby.com. Follow Amber Elby on Twitter @amberelby

TRIGGER WARNING   This text contains instances of abusive
behavior, thoughts of self-harm, and suicidal tendencies that
parallel events described in William Shakespeare's plays. If you or
someone you know need help, please visit nimh.nih.gov or reach
out to your local mental health services. You are loved.

TABLE OF CONTENTS

Double, double, toile and trouble;
Fire burne, and Cauldron bubble.

~William Shakespeare (1564-1616), *Macbeth*
Witches' Chant, Act 4, Scene 1
First Folio, 1623

Chapter One: Perchance to Dream

Dreng saw nothing. Rather, he could not see. All was black, an inky curtain thrown over reality. He knew Alda, so close to him moments ago as floodwater rushed into the cottage, should be nearby. So he reached for her.

Yet his fingers grasped only air.

He felt a brief wash of panic, like being swept under waves, but he pushed the fear into the pit of his stomach and struggled to his feet. Surely there was an explanation. Something real in this impossible situation.

Had he been transported somehow?

Knocked out by the flood and dreaming?

Or dead?

For a terrifying moment, Dreng wondered if he had been taken down into the vast depths of the beyond, to some ancient place of demons and ghosts and unimaginable tortures.

But he felt no immortal anguish. And he could *feel*: the hard stone at his feet, the chill prickling his arms, the damp shiver on his neck. The rough-woven fabric of his clothes, the river's water in his hair and leather boots. Prince Hamlet's signet ring, tight on his finger. The damp pages of the miniature spell book within his leather belt, pressed against his waist. The ground was solid, too. Wet and cold. There was a smell, like stale water. Fresh water. Mold and mildew. Rust. And dripping.

Finally, he drew a breath. "Alda?" The word echoed. "Alda, where are you?"

No answer.

He waited for footsteps, breathing, something worse, anything to indicate that he was not alone.

All was still.

He must have been transported somewhere, here, to this so solid place.

With a jolt he remembered the bubble, the glimmering sphere that he had held in the cottage, the object that Alda said could move one through time and place.

That thing had surely vanished both Alda and him.

But where was the mysterious bubble now?

Gone.

Most likely, it was with Alda. Elsewhere. But how?

He focused his mind, remembering what he could.

Days before — days, or weeks — he had been in the fairies' realm. Subjected to the whims of the tyrant queen. Threatened by the king. Given a sword and wounded by a dagger. The poison. The recovery. The pain in his shoulder remained sharp, but less intense.

If he had time, he could fully heal. But now, well, perhaps time was all he had. Too much time, alone. Or too little.

He thought back to Alda's cottage and the brief calm,

like an eye of a storm. Then turmoil, an emotional tempest. His father's ghost. A flood. The cauldron's bubble, made and used and… lost.

Before that, before all that, he had placed his wife's body in a frozen pool.

Wife. What else could he call her? Not *Miranda*, not any more. Not after what he learned from Alda. But *Sycorax* felt wrong. It was an evil name. The moniker of one bent on destruction.

But were Alda's words in the cottage true? Were Miranda and Sycorax one in the same, the kind maiden and the fiery summoner?

What could he believe? *Whom* could he believe? Alda, a stranger he met only in flashes, darting in and out of his life, complicating and risking it? Or the woman he knew as his wife, the young islander once loved and once loving, but who also brought a cavern crumbling down around them as her past came to light?

Then he remembered. The stench. The dripping. The darkness. The cave.

He was in a cave. But it was not the same vast cavern on the enchanted island, not with the lights and illuminated walls that collapsed as his trust was shattered.

Now, there were no gemstones, no way to find focus. No vision.

But Dreng could not be still. He had to move, to

escape, to save himself, at least.

He took a tentative step, pain shooting from his leg to his shoulder. Then another, holding his unseen hands before him. Then a third, and he heard a clink like glass upon the ground.

He had kicked something, something small, so he knelt and reached and felt with his fingertips until his hand connected on an object other than damp stones.

He examined the thing in his palm, feeling its surface. Smooth. Small, yet heavy. A perfect sphere. No. Half of a sphere.

It was the cauldron's bubble. Cleaved in twain. One of two halves.

The other part, he suspected, was with Alda. But where was she?

He fumbled to place the broken orb in his pocket, its fabric threadbare and damp. It was safe, he hoped.

Hope.

Again, he took a tentative step. Then he paused and listened.

Laughter, sudden and short. Dreng cocked his head, listening. Again. No, not laughter. A cackle. Malicious.

It grew in a crescendo. No, not louder. Closer.

Dreng knew in his heart of hearts that it was not safe. Whoever was
laughing in this place of absolute darkness could be

nothing but malevolent. Yet he followed the noise, groping in the dark, his arms outstretched before him.

Then he felt warm. No, not warm. Less chilled. The smell dissipated. The moisture dried. The rocks below his feet gave way to — to nothing.

And there was light, a green glow in the distance.

But there was nothing else. Only Dreng, his heartbeat, and the distant light. The rest was black, empty.

This was somewhere else. Somewhere new. Not the lightless cave where he so suddenly appeared after the flood. This was a place of pure blackness. A void.

In a breath, Dreng knew where he was. This was the place of which he had been told, the place he could not believe. A place of spirits and of nothing. Netherfeld.

The laughter returned, sudden and overpowering. Not a single voice, but a chorus. A cacophony.

And three figures appeared, three women robed in black, draping silk, silhouetted against the glowing horizon. Laughing and tossing the tangles of dark hair on their heads, their faces obscured by shadows and beards.

Dreng backed away, but it was too late. He was seen.

The figures moved closer, their faces clearer. Dreng knew them somehow, distantly, in some memory that had been pressed below the surface of his thoughts. They were familiar.

And he knew they were dangerous.

"The waters worked, sister."

"And washed what we wished."

"Whisked what we wished for."

He stilled his instincts and stopped backing away.
His feet held firm, even if his heart was not.

He stuttered, "Who, who are you?"

"A poor introduction."

"A name for a name."

"Give us yours first, boy."

They spoke quickly, one voice bleeding into the next.

He gulped and whispered, "Dreng."

"A lie."

"But he believes it."

"No, he knows."

"He did not."

"Now knows."

"Now, and then."

"So speak the truth."

They paused, waiting.

And he tried to hold his tongue, but the words felt
forced from his throat. For the first time, Dreng parted
his lips to speak his name, his true name, the name that
his father's ghost had told him outside Alda's cottage, a
name that felt simultaneously foreign and familiar yet,
somehow, ill fitting. Like an assigned part within a play.

"Thomas." He gulped. "Thomas Chatterton."

The women spoke together, ignoring Dreng. He stood awkwardly, trying to unravel their thread of words.

"Do we know?"

"Some."

"More."

"It is all and nothing."

"Nothing to us."

"All to him."

"That is all?"

"Enough."

"'Tis not."

"And him?"

"Nothing."

"To us?"

"No, some."

"Yes, more."

"His name?"

"His?"

"What's in a name?"

"A boy by any other."

"Is still a boy."

"This, the boy."

"Still, the boy."

"I am not a boy," Dreng interjected. He thought of Caliban, of his insults. These women — no, creatures — were cut from the same cloth. "Tell me your names." He strained to sound more confident than he felt, but his voice cracked on the final consonant.

"Ask a question."

Dreng narrowed his eyes, "Who are you?"

"Us."

"We are us."

"We are three."

"No, what are your names?" Dreng's eyes flitted from one face to the next. The strange women were nearly indistinguishable, different only in height.

"Morta."

"Decima."

"Nona."

"But that is not *the* question."

Before Dreng could stop himself, he blurted, "*What* are you?"

"Weyward."

"Weird."

"Sisters."

"Witches."

And Dreng remembered. That night, so many years ago, amid the colored lightning that surrounded his father's ship, *The Tyger,* amid the chaos and the rain and the screams of pain, he had heard voices. A chant. A spell. And laughter.

Their laughter.

These were the witches who had killed his father. He had found them, at last.

A brief smile flashed across Dreng's face, despite his attempt to conceal the sudden joy he felt at this discovery of the witches. No, not joy. Relief. "I know you."

The tallest laughed at his words, the sound high and shrill. "You know so little."

"His false heart knows."

"Heartless."

"Broken."

Dreng clenched his fists. Should he fear these creatures? Their powers? "What do you want?"

"A word."

"Some."

"Words."

"Words."

Dreng felt his nails dig into his palms as he asked, "What words?"

"Yours."

"You speak by the book."

"But they are yours *only now*."

"Ours soon."

Dreng decided that he had seen and survived worse and suppressed his fear. He drew a breath and blurted, "Then let us trade words for words. I know you murdered my father. With some spell or charm. But why?"

They turned toward one another and spoke in loud whispers, seeming to ignore him as they conspired.

"He is still so little."

"But fierce."

"Should we tell him, sisters?"

"Or let him grope in the dark?"

They turned their eerily beautiful faces to him, and the shortest smirked. "Knowledge for knowledge, boy."

"Tell me of my father."

"He is dead." More laughter.

Dreng felt the hair on his neck stand on end. "By your hand."

"By our words."

"Our words and a blow."

"You tried to kill me." Dreng felt sweat bead on his brow.

"Kill?"

"Never."

"You were in the way."

"Collateral, some would say."

"But you stole from us."

"That night."

"On *The Tyger*."

Dreng reflexively reached for a weapon, but he was unarmed. "I am not a thief."

"A man of character."

"A pirate of principle."

"I am not a pirate," he hissed.

"And a liar."

"Yet I am no fool." Dreng crossed his arms and tried to stand taller. "I will give you more of my words. The words that you want. If you tell me why you attacked our ship."

The witches stopped circling and stared, unblinking. He guessed the meaning of their sudden silence. He had hit upon the vein.

"Tell me of my father's death, and I will give you what you want. Freely."

"We could take it now, boy." The witch sneered.

"Why not tell him, sister?"

"It matters not to us."

"But will it pain him?"

"With certainty."

"Then do."

The shortest witch reached within her black robes and withdrew a sphere of water. It hovered above her palm as she whispered into it, spat on its surface, and threw it to the black void at Dreng's feet.

The liquid expanded into a pool that shone like a looking glass. Upon its surface, the reflection of a figure appeared: a young woman with rosy cheeks, carrying a basket. Her arms tanned and muscular as she walked a dirt path at the base of a barren hill. She looked to the

ground with a tear in her eye. Her face was serene yet
forlorn. No, sad. And familiar.

Her aspect was like a painting from a memory,
distant and almost
magical. Dreng grappled with his mind, weaving images
until his past became more clear. A tapestry formed from
his thoughts.

And he realized it was the face of his mother.

As he watched the image in the water, he wanted to
reach for her. To save her. But shadows descended.
Three cloaked figures surrounded her, performing a kind
of animalistic dance. They were witches — these same
witches — pulling at his mother's dark hair and ragged
dress, ripping the basket from her hands and scattering
its contents across the muddy earth.

Colored lights flashed, and the young woman fell to
the ground. The witches in the watery image took the
basket and ascended into the foggy sky.

Dreng looked up, tears obscuring his vision. "Did
you kill her?"

Silence.

He looked again to the water. The woman did not
move. Finally, he dashed its surface, and the pool
evaporated in a burst of steam.

Dreng faced the three sisters, his voice shaking in
anger. "You did, you killed her. And why? For what?" He

drew a breath, waiting. "What was in the basket?"

The mid-height sister snickered. "Chestnuts."

"Chestnuts? You took her life for, for chestnuts?"

"She would not share."

"Said they were for her husband."

"On *The Tyger*."

"Near Aleppo."

"Coming home, soon."

"But she had stolen the nuts."

"From our tree."

"Thief."

"Death to thieves."

Dreng's mind whirled, fitting together pieces of his past. "So you three sent a spell to my father as well? To our ship."

"A curse."

"To sleep."

"To waste."

"To die."

"But not yet."

A strange calm washed over the witches, and their eyes focused on something beyond Dreng, something far away. He thought for a moment that they spoke to one another, not to him, as their whispered voices lost their rough edges and smoothly blended together. As one witch spoke, another started:

"You, Thomas Chatterton, will live a life. Yet a lie. A full life. Until you perish. Atop a crimson, singing mountain. As it burns."

Dreng had heard tales of prophecy, of supernatural beings whispering omens to men at sea. Was this such? If so, he would not die today, now. He took a breath to screw his courage as he rolled up his sleeve, revealing the red scar that coursed from his chest to his arm. "You did this."

The sisters' focus snapped back to him. They did not look at his scar but instead gazed into his eyes.

"We have told."

"Given you our words."

"So now you give."

"Give, give!"

Goosepimples formed upon Dreng's neck. "Give what? What words do you want?"

"Nothing."

"Nothing."

"Nothing that you can live without."

And before Dreng could flee, their wiry hands were upon him.

Chapter Two: Such Stuff as Dreams

Alda stared into her palm, her fingers shaking. The cauldron's bubble was broken. In half. Useless.

Dreng was gone, again.

And she was alone. Again.

But where?

Inside a palace, glittering and golden. Emerald-tinged light filtered down from some unseen source high above. All was grand. Gilded. Every candlestick, chair, even a long, sturdy table were encrusted with shining jewels and precious metals. Tapestries adorned the walls, images of ancient gods in love and battle, and a fireplace surrounded by glittering tiles that sparkled around gold-green flames.

Alda had never seen such glorious wealth, such excess. Whoever inhabited this place was powerful. Alda also hoped they were benevolent.

She carefully tucked the broken bubble into her sock as she explored her surroundings. There appeared to be no windows and no door. Only the tapestry-clad walls and great hearth.

She was trapped.

So she turned to the grand table that stretched through the center of the circular room, its surface scattered with books. Alda tried to read their covers, but all were in Latin or Greek or other ancient tongues.

As she studied them, several marbled volumes materialized before her eyes. *Life of Lord Byron*, one of her grandmother's beloved poets. She opened the top book and read, "So we'll go no more a-roving, so late into the night, though the heart be still as loving, and the moon be still as bright. For the sword outwears its sheath, and the soul wears out the breast, and the heart must pause to breathe, and love itself have rest." She did not read the final stanza as her words echoed disconcertingly. It sounded strangely like eavesdroppers calling back from above.

As Alda closed the book, the volumes vanished. So she turned her attention instead to the tapestries. She recognized Athena from her illustrated mythologies, with her owl and helmet. Zeus with his lightning bolt. Hera with her crown and staff, so much like the one held by Prospero.

At the recollection, Alda's mind filled with questions. What could have created this place, with its materializing books and extravagant furnishings? Or rather, *who* could have created it?

As if on cue, a tapestry fluttered. Alda stepped back, clutching a chair that might serve as a weapon if violence came. But the tapestry parted to reveal a second chamber, small with stone walls and narrow windows that showed only black night beyond. And in the threshold of this lonely room was a familiar figure.

"Ophelia!" Alda stepped toward her, relief flooding

her face. "I thought the worst, that you were taken by the witches or, or —"

"Ophelia?" The young, red-haired woman did not share Alda's joy at their reunion. Her eyes revealed some inner turmoil, her mouth twitching between a forced smile and a sneer. "That is what I was once called. Once, before you abandoned me in this place of nothing. But why dwell in the past? Here, sit." It was clearly a command, not a request.

Alda felt her knees buckle and slipped into a curved-leg chair as Ophelia continued, her voice rising into a shrill crescendo, "I, too, had questions at the start, Alda. Foremost: why? Why did you escape into the land beyond and leave me to endure the witches' fury?"

"It was an accident. I thought, I thought that you would —" The red-haired woman raised her hand, and Alda felt her throat close.

"Old excuses! Old, and tired." She sighed. "And when you returned, after so much time had passed, why did you imprison me in this gilded cage?"

"Cage?" Alda paused and wondered, "Are we in Netherfeld?"

Ophelia slapped her hand on the table, sending pages swirling into the air with supernatural force. "Do not play the innocent! It does not suit you."

Alda tried to stand, to confront her, but she was

trapped. Her hands could not lift from the chair's ornate arms, and her torso could not rise from its seat. But she summoned the courage to object, "No, I would not do that! I did not imprison you!" She took several breaths and steadied her tone, "Why would you think that I did?" Her voice broke on the final word as she thought of several, including the witches, whom she might throw in a dungeon.

Alda swallowed and continued, "Ophelia, I —"

"No! That is not my name. Not *now*."

And Alda realized that this was not Ophelia, not the girl she knew before. This was someone else. This was a later version of the young mother, alone and trapped and born anew. Dangerous. This was Sycorax, the woman Ophelia would become. The woman who wanted to kill Alda.

"Sycorax? What happened when I was gone?"

The sorceress laughed. "Ah, you have forgotten." A wry smile flashed across her face. "Now, now, now, in this petty place I record my time." She motioned to a book that flew open, revealing a journal with calligraphic handwriting. "Light, candle!" She snapped her fingers, and a candelabra burst into sparkling flames. "No more shadows, now. Only a tale of sound and fury."

The young woman paced around the table and stopped as she faced Alda, her eyes aflame and hair lifting in some unseen breeze as she ran her finger over the journal's pages.

As Alda watched, a scene formed before her, lighted figures in miniature moving across the book's faded surface. Dollhouse toys come to life, like costumed players on a diminutive stage.

Like those Prospero had shown to her on the island.

Ophelia — no, Sycorax — curved her finger in the air, and Alda recognized the scene: a young woman with red hair, with an infant clasped to her chest, lights shooting from one hand, holding back three cloaked figures, the witches.

Alda had seen this before she had passed through the tree into Fairy Land and, in doing so, abandoned the young mother she called Ophelia in Netherfeld with her infant son, Hamnet.

"This is the story of my creation." Alda's companion narrated the scene. "Of course it began much earlier, with my Hamlet's madness and my early devotion to the weird sisters, but I confided that secret already." The young woman paced, wringing her hands. "After you left, I was trapped here, with my son, surrounded by the witches who had, had —"

Alda's companion paused, searching for the right word, "Who had led to my Hamlet's downfall. And mine. And they were here, but they did not seem to know me, as if I was a stranger. As if they had not met me. Not yet."

She stopped and stared directly at Alda, her eyes sparkling. "I met them before they had met me. In their past. So I told them I was Sycorax, a powerful summoner. And that my son was named Caliban and was rightful heir to a realm of magic." She lowered her voice menacingly, "And that I bowed to no one."

The witches' figures cowered as she spoke, their images flickering like a sputtering candle. "I told them to let me be free. They agreed, if I would let them live. So they transported us onto an enchanted island."

The scene evaporated, and a new setting appeared. Alda recognized the banks of the Stream of Consciousness amid the bowing trees and greenery of Prospero's island. "My son was whole, complete for the first time in the real world, out of this wretched plane where he was born. But I — I was not."

A shadow appeared against the calm surface of the water. The figure of a woman, a black silhouette, holding a too-solid infant. The images evaporated as the young woman said, "He grew, yet I was fading. My body had died, you see, drowned, and I was merely a walking shadow. A shade."

She sighed, "Years passed. I taught my son some magic, what I could, but I was only a figment. Not of the earth. Not tied to it. Weak. And then one day, a sorcerer arrived, a man called Prospero." The storyteller's eyes met Alda's as she warned, "If you ever meet him, do not trust him."

Alda thought back to Prospero's story of his past. Sycorax, dark-haired and power-hungry. Caliban, a grotesque monster. Miranda, a helpless victim. And the old sorcerer himself, the hero of magic and savior of the island.

Who lied, Sycorax or Prospero? A knot formed in Alda's throat as she realized the answer was, most likely, both.

Sycorax waved her fingers, and more figures appeared. The robed man that Alda recognized as Prospero, and a girl with fair, blonde hair. It was Miranda, Alda knew, but she remained silent.

"The old man wanted only power. Magic. Knowledge. To control what was not his. First, he commanded my help, my spells. I yielded what I could, but he wanted more." The figures interacted: the boy and girl played and danced while the robed man bent threateningly over the female shadow.

Sycorax took a deep breath and continued, "The sorcerer was so trapped in his mind that he could not understand the world around him. Not nature or beauty or, especially, love." The boy and girl embraced. "So when my son and his daughter —" She choked back a sob. "The old man cursed my boy. And banished me here. To this empty realm."

Alda wanted to ask more questions, to know more fully about Prospero and Miranda and also Ariel, but she held her tongue, silently waiting for her companion to finish the tale, not wanting to reveal what she already knew.

With a snap, the figures vanished. Sycorax wiped either sweat or tears from her face as she murmured, "Then you came. And found me here, in Netherfeld. But you, too, did not know me."

Alda watched as a version of herself, dressed in the black clothes of her grandmother's mourning, appeared suddenly above the page. Sycorax waved her hand, and it vanished.

Alda gasped, "What happened? What did I do?"

Sycorax stood taller and choked on a laugh. "You *know*."

Alda shook her head as her eyes filled with frustrated tears. "But I don't remember!"

Laughter erupted from Sycorax's lips, shrill and long and echoing in the space above.

"You are always the *ingénue*, Alda. Never in control. Pushed and pulled like foam atop the ocean during a storm." Sycorax filled her words with deep and hateful wrath.

Alda shuddered, "Whatever happened, I am certain I can help you fix it."

"Here is your chance." She raised her arms, motioning to the palace around her, and let them fall helplessly at her sides.

"I don't understand."

"Undo what you have done, Alda. Release me."

"From what?"

Again, Sycorax slapped the table. Pages flew in a whirl of parchment, hitting the tapestries and floating like feathers to the marble floor. She spoke slowly, enunciating each word. "From this prison you built for me."

Alda tried once more to rise from her chair, but she was still held tightly to its surface. "This is surely not a prison! And you were not trapped here for so long. I saw you on the island several months ago, with Caliban and Dreng."

A shadow seemed to fall across Sycorax's face. "Who is Dreng?"

Alda stammered, "The boy from the ship. Shipwrecked. You, you —" She could not finish. The confusion in Sycorax's eyes was unsettling. "How do you not know your own husband?"

"Husband?" She laughed, a sound of joy this time. "Surely not."

"Yes, you married him the night you defeated Prospero. The night you drove me from the island. Surely you must remember."

"Remember?" Sycorax again paced and rubbed her hands anxiously. "Yes, I will remember. But that has not yet happened." A smile held strong on her lips. "But I will defeat him, you say? Defeat Prospero?"

Alda nodded, uncertain how much more to reveal.

The bubble had apparently taken her to Sycorax's past, into the time between when she was Ophelia and when she took control of Miranda's body on the island.

This was not the Ophelia that Alda knew nor the Sycorax she would later meet. This was someone else. A new form.

And despite being trapped in the extraordinary palace with red-haired Sycorax, despite being trapped in a realm with no time and no form, Alda remembered a conversation with her grandmother, many years before, as the older woman taught her how to transform skeins of yarn into scarves and blankets.

Alda remembered that the cottage was especially cold that winter, and she shivered as she watched her grandmother.

"No, twist it this way, dear, and hold this needle thus." Her grandmother was patient, but Alda was not.

"I'll never learn, Gramma!" Alda's voice was high with youth and frustration. "This will take forever."

"No, not forever. But it will take time." Her grandmother set aside the knitting needles and the ball of coarse, brown wool as she embraced young Alda. Over her shoulder, Alda stared at the wooden needles in the candlelight and tried to calm herself as her grandmother soothed, "You know, time is a funny thing. For you, it is like the needles: straight with a knob and a point, a beginning and an end. But the time of others, the way you see them, is like the yarn. It is full of loops and twists and turns that only sometimes cross the needle."

Alda was calmer now, able to think. "Is this a riddle?"

"In a way." Her grandmother examined her eyes. "You know the novel I am reading, about the artist who ran away to live in the abandoned mansion, the book with the split binding?"

Alda knew the volume and nodded, so Gramma continued, "It was written over fifty years ago, and the woman who wrote it has since died. But to me, that book is now. I am reading something from the past but in my present." She held the yarn deftly in her fingers and twisted it over the tip of a needle, showing how the wood and wool seemed to intersect. "And I read that novel before, when I was younger, so that was another time it crossed my straight line." Again, she looped the yarn. "And someday, after I am gone, you will read that book." She picked up the second needle. "And it will be the author's past, and my past, and your present, all intersecting." She twisted the wool and crossed the needles, and soon an entire row was complete.

"We all have our own time-needles, Alda. Our perception is straight. But the world around us loops and twists and doubles back. Sometimes, it is even cut and retied with a new yarn."

Watching her, Alda commented, "That is a silly riddle." But she likewise picked up her knitting and mimicked her grandmother until, sooner than she expected, she had the beginning of a scarf.

Now, in Alda's present in Netherfeld, and Sycorax's past in Netherfeld, Alda understood the analogy:

People likewise crossed paths and crossed time, as did the yarn and needles.

Alda thought of Dreng, how he had grown up during her time with the witches on the moor when she had barely aged. Of how she had met Ophelia, a young mother who later became Sycorax. Of the babe Hamnet, whom she had known as the monster Caliban, who later transformed into a beautiful young man. Of the woman she knew as Sycorax, this woman, who did not yet know of the wicked deeds she would perform.

These lives of others were the yarn, crossing and intertwining, at times overlapping. And Alda's life was the needle, straight and linear.

Sycorax snapped her fingers, and Alda's mind returned to the present as the chair on which she sat collapsed into splinters beneath her. Alda stood awkwardly as the fiery woman caught her wrist. "You will help me escape, Alda. You will undo this prison you have erected and free me into the world beyond, your world, where I can fulfill my duty and reclaim my island."

Alda recoiled as the fingernails dug into her wrist like talons. She did not know what to do, how to save herself and help Sycorax. If she *should* help Sycorax. But now, she had no choice, or rather only small and rotten choices. So she nodded weakly.

What else could she do?

Chapter Three: Night's Black Agents

Dreng felt weak as the weird sisters loomed above him. Exhausted. Drained. His heartbeat was a whisper as a stream of light connected his scar to the witches' fingers.

Could he run? If so, where? But he could not stand.

Could he fight? With what? But he could not raise his arms.

Could he live?

Not for long.

Whatever they were taking from him, whatever they were tapping from his body, was something that he could not live without.

So he pleaded with the strange sisters, his voice coming in whispers and gasps. "Let me help you! Whatever you need, whatever task, I offer my aid." He searched their blank, unfeeling eyes and forced out, "I can read, read magical tongues. I can be of service —"

"You can do as we."

"This skill is ours."

"Not yours."

"And ours again."

The yellow rope of light intensified, pulsating in its increasing energy.

Dreng's heart felt cold, as if seawater pressed against his organs. One blink, perhaps two, was all that remained.

With a breath — his last — he let loose a scream like a baited bear, deep and animalistic. Instinctual.

A pause. A moment suspended in time that seemed at once an eternity and a heartbeat.

A flash like sunlight. Heat. And then a suffocating blow. Dreng's face and arms wrapped, pinned, held beneath a fabric net from which he could not break free.

Then all was quiet. Apart from the ringing in his ears.

Dreng sat upright and pushed a blanket from his head. As his ears pounded and limbs tingled, he squinted into the gloom.

A slim form was silhouetted against the horizon's dim, green light. The figure replaced a sword on its belt as it approached Dreng.

"Who are you?"

"*Deus ex machina*, it would appear." Dreng recognized the familiar sneer as his companion crouched at his side.

"Caliban?"

"I, in this analogy, am the god. You are the machine. And a broken one at that."

Broken, indeed. Throbbing ache from his too-recent injury in Fairy Land. And now, the damage caused by the witches... But Dreng suppressed the pain, as he had so many times at sea.

His jaw clenched against his will as he asked, "How did you find me?"

The beautiful youth tore off a corner of his shirt and gently touched the blood that trickled from Dreng's scar. "Find *you*? No. I found the witches. You simply had the good luck, or the misfortune, to be with them when I did."

Dreng struggled to stand, but his knees buckled. Caliban caught him and continued, "You must wear the cloak, friend. It will protect you."

A cloak, not a net or a blanket, had covered his head. The sapphire blue cloak that Caliban had fished from the sea before they set forth into Fairy Land. "Those witches are up to something, something wicked. I've been on their trail, and when I saw them ensnare you —"

"You were here? Watching, while they were —" Dreng pushed him away and steadied his feet. "While they were killing me?"

"I intervened before they succeeded, of course."

"Barely."

"Surely that is worth something."

"Little more than nothing." Dreng examined the wound on his chest, the dark circle around it that smelled of cooked meat.

Caliban followed his gaze, his eyes filled with concern. "You should not deal with those devils."

Dreng self-consciously covered the wound with his shirt. To his surprise, it did not hurt. Rather, it did not feel. "What do they want?"

"Apart from killing you?"

"Apart from taking the supposed something," Dreng corrected.

"Of course. The *something*." Caliban's words were heavy with sarcasm.

"What is it?"

"*It* is of great importance."

Dreng tried to conceal his smile. "You do not know either."

"I know more than you."

"Such as?"

"I know where we are."

"As do I. Netherfeld."

Caliban scoffed, "But what is Netherfeld?"

Dreng shook his head, so Caliban continued, "When I was a child, my mother told me of a realm of pure magic. Where one could imagine a lion, and a lion would appear. Where the impossible could happen, simply from one's thoughts. That it was once lush and populated with thousands of magical creatures. Then witches came. And the creatures scattered. The fairies, to their world. We to ours. And others, so many others, to different, faraway realms. The world of pure magic became black. Void. And, if the witches have their way, they will do to our world what they did to Netherfeld." His voice broke, and he continued, "I have startled them away, for now, but they will return soon enough. We must move apace."

Caliban turned, and Dreng followed his footsteps, his limbs aching with exhaustion. "How can we stop them?" Dreng's voice trembled.

"We cannot."

"Then what will we do?"

"Die, perhaps."

Caliban led the way briskly, and Dreng trotted painfully after him. After too many minutes of silence, Dreng grew weary of walking through the nothing with his moody companion. He had questions — too many questions — but doubted that Caliban would answer any. Still, he tried, "How did you get here?"

"Through a tree. And several detours and distractions. And a loss, but — Let us speak of the present, not the past."

"Fine. Then what of me? What did the witches want?"

The two walked in silence for a dozen or more paces, through the nothing of Netherfeld. Dreng, wrapped in the blue cloak. Caliban, nervously fidgeting with the hilt of his sword.

After what felt like too long, Caliban relented, "Your wife told me there was something in you that was different."

Dreng's heart sank to his feet. He could not speak of Miranda — no, Sycorax — not now, not after so much with Alda in the cottage, so he remained silent.

Caliban seemed to grope for words, speaking slowly, "You have a gift. No, a curse. No. That is not right either." He looked at his feet and slowed his pace. "You have an ability."

"Ability? Like swordplay?"

"No, something innate. Like an intuition. Or a power. Yes, a power."

"What power?"

"They said they wanted words, yes? You have the power of speech." Caliban laughed. Dreng did not.

But he thought about the cauldron's bubble. How his words helped to create it.

"As the witches said, you stole this power. It somehow bonded with you that night on the ship."

"How?"

To Dreng's surprise, Caliban stopped and studied him for several heartbeats before parting the cloak and lifting Dreng's shirt to reveal the scar. "They left their mark on you. A symbol of magic. Like a rune or sigil."

"Was it intentional?"

"We mortals cannot guess." He walked again, purposefully toward some unknown destination. "We merely see the present and the shadows of the past. Those dark and midnight hags see more."

"More? Then how can we stop them?"

"More, but not all."

Dreng considered. "Are they gods?"

"Ancient, of a sort. Primordial. Of the chaos, before worlds."

"How do you know?"

Caliban grinned. "Do you not trust me?"

Dreng started to respond but bit his tongue. He was alone here, confused, torn from Alda and all that he knew. Alone and in the dark, most literally. He did not need to cause offense and risk what little safety he had in the company of his companion.

"The witches, they want to kill me?"

Caliban laughed, "Don't we all?"

Dreng scowled, "Then why have they not done so before now?"

Caliban stopped walking and considered. "As a boy, you were nothing to them. Perhaps they forgot about you, or perhaps they were preoccupied elsewhere. Regardless, once you were on my island, you were safe."

"Why?"

"The spells. My mother's. Prospero's. The island was protected. Later, in the realm of the fairies, you were likewise safe. But when we were at sea —"

"Mermaids."

Caliban nodded. "Sea witches, rather, some cousins of those you met moments past."

"But we escaped."

"They are lesser than these."

"How do you know of these things?" Dreng's brow furrowed with suspicion.

Caliban only laughed. "I am the son of a prince. And a witch."

It was an echo of the words spoken on the raft. Familiar but altered. "If that's so, then I'm descended from Neptune himself." Dreng's tone dripped with sarcasm.

But Caliban was serious. "I jest not. I expected you to know by now, but you are not the brightest star in the heavens." He cleared his throat and pulled himself up to his full height. "I, Caliban, was by birth called Hamnet. Son of Hamlet, Prince of Denmark."

 Dreng laughed. "He had no son. He never spoke of one." Dreng had suspected a resemblance between Caliban and the Danish prince before, after their raft had been destroyed, but now, to hear such a connection spoken aloud — it was surely the stuff of fantasy.

"He did not know. I was a posthumous child. Born after my mother died."

Nonsense. Dreng scoffed, "Do not continue this, this poor joke. I knew him."

"Skepticism does not become you."

"Then speak truth."

"Truth? None of this matters." Caliban waved his hand as if swatting a fly from his face. "There are more pressing worries at present."

The two walked in silence for some minutes. Dreng began to feel something like suspicion, then regret, and his face burned. What if Caliban was indeed Hamlet's son?

Dreng finally spoke first, his tone soft. "How did you defeat the witches here, today?"

"With all of my strength. I cannot do so again." The beautiful youth paused and added, "How many days did you spend with your witch?"

"My witch?" Dreng paused. "Alda?"

Caliban nodded soberly.

Dreng cleared his throat and continued, "Days. A week. I am not certain."

"Then she is more powerful than I anticipated, if the witches did not find you with her. We will need her help." Caliban again stopped. "Where is she?"

Dreng bit his lip. "I do not know."

Chapter Four: Fabric of Vision

Alda's wrist bled as Sycorax pulled her to a gilded wall and thrust her face against its bejeweled surface. Alda tried to back away, but the summoner's other hand held her head tight as her knee jabbed into Alda's spine. She could not move.

"This, this prison is from you! You did this, Alda! You are my jailor!" Sycorax released her, and Alda crumbled to the ground. "Get up!"

Alda struggled to find her feet but lost her balance. Sycorax impatiently grabbed her raven hair and hoisted her to full height. She kept a tight hold on her locks as she commanded, "Make it vanish!"

Alda felt tears on her face but resolution in her heart. She would not budge. "No!" If she had constructed this place for Sycorax, to hold her here against her will, then she must not destroy it now.

Even if Alda could no longer remember building it, or why it was created.

Sycorax released Alda's hair as she paced toward the far end of the room. Alda steadied herself and stood tall, her chin high and defiant like an armored warrior in one of her stereopticon cards.

When Sycorax turned again toward her, her face was calm and smiling. Alda stepped back as the summoner cooed, "We were friends once, Alda. We built a city, a vast city beyond these walls. It glowed a beautiful green, the same color as these lights." She looked to the ceiling above. "And we were happy, you and I. Queens. Friends."

Her tone darkened. "But then you changed, Alda. You heard whispers of Prospero's lies and took his side against me. Then you imprisoned me here. And vanished. And all these years — years? who knows time in this place? — I have waited for you. For your help." Again, she smiled. But there was no kindness in her eyes.

Alda subconsciously backed away as her companion spoke and was suddenly aware that her shoulders touched the golden threads of an intricate tapestry. She turned only to see Medusa's head smiling down at her, held in the hand of victorious Perseus. She stepped away, and Sycorax joined her side.

"You and I wove these, Alda, together. As I said, we were like sisters. Our looms here in Netherfeld were our minds, and we could spin gold into anything with simply our thoughts." She took Alda's hand reassuringly but then held tight as Alda tried to pull away. "We can be friends again. Tear down these walls, Alda. Burn the whole tower down. Let me be free again."

Alda reclaimed her hand and stepped back toward the tapestry. Again, "No!"

Sycorax calmly eyed her as she stepped past Alda

and parted the tapestry, revealing a solid wall adorned with a simple spiral.

Alda recognized it immediately. A witch-trap. The magical symbol that could entrap and torture witches.

Sycorax spoke again, her voice like an angry mistress scolding an unruly child, as she repeated, "You did this, Alda. You placed these here, encircling my tower. To keep me in place. To trap me. But they can trap you, too. Trap you, and worse." She paused. "So help me destroy them, or I will deal much worse."

As Alda looked from the summoner to the spiral, her thoughts sped through possibilities. She could release Sycorax, yes, and face the consequences of unleashing evil. Or perhaps Sycorax was sincere. A friend. And all would be well. Or Alda could resign herself to the trap. She had been ensnared by one before, in the Canyon. And although she might die in the real world from the elements or starvation, she faced no such danger in Netherfeld. Only weariness and, perhaps, torture. She expected she could withstand both.

And, perhaps, Sycorax was bluffing. She was trapped here, after all. Seemingly helpless.

Alda bit her lip, thinking. Then, while she weighed her options, Alda heard a whisper. Faint at first. Distant. And then the spiral erupted in a green light, its beams ricocheting from the room's countless jewels.

Alda was momentarily blinded, and Sycorax held her hand before her eyes to block the rays. The voices grew louder. More distinct. Closer.

"Against the wall." Faint, commanding.

"What now?" Worried and confused.

And Alda recognized their tones, so she turned to Sycorax, her eyes wide. "You must touch the spiral."

"No! That is surely death." The summoner's voice cracked with fear. "This is a trick."

More sounds. The first voice continued, a string of words muttered incoherently. And Alda knew the sound.

"Sycorax, that boy calling you from the other side is your son. He is performing some kind of spell for you to enter the island. If you follow his call, you will survive."

"How do you know?"

Alda took a deep breath and appeared as confident as she could. "Because it has already happened."

This was Alda's chance. An opportunity to escape. To overpower her captor. And, if her supposition was correct, to align her past with her present.

Alda held her breath as Sycorax bent toward the symbol, listening as she kept one hand on the tapestry. After a moment, she held a finger tentatively toward the spiral, like a child daring herself to touch a boiling kettle, but then recoiled. "I cannot. Alda, I don't —"

But Alda did not hear the final words. As Sycorax

turned away from the symbol, Alda lunged and pushed her toward its glowing surface.

A sputter of sparks, like electric lights snapping suddenly out. A cloud of dark smoke. When it cleared, nothing. The spiral was gone. Sycorax was gone. And the room had lost its green glow.

The walls themselves were less radiant, almost dull. Like a faded photograph. And as Alda watched, the gilded room disappeared.

At first it was gradual, like fog lifting after sunrise. Then more violent: golden stones crumbling, jewels bursting, metal twisting and bending as colored lights streaked through the air above. Alda dove beneath the table and pulled a fallen tapestry over her shoulders as the tower collapsed around her.

Rather, it did not collapse. It simply vanished. Alda first felt the tapestry grow cold and quickly realized she was grasping only her own palms. Then the table shifted to one side and fell like a coin into an invisible well, vanishing into the enveloping dark.

Soon Alda was alone again in the black, silent void of Netherfeld.

She stood and pressed her shaking palms together. Sycorax was gone, thrust onto the island with Dreng and Caliban. Into Alda's past. The tower was likewise vanished, somehow.

Alda surveyed the space beneath her feet. There was no indication of a foundation, no trace of the walls that had so recently enclosed the summoner. It was as if it had never existed.

Yet there was life, still. Or rather movement.

Spirits stirred above, lifting like wafting smoke from a dying flame. Slow and thin at first, then faster. Their numbers swelled, and Alda was surrounded by dancing swirls of light and color, their luminescent hues of green and blue dazzling her eyes.

And, like on Prospero's island, the spirits spoke to her. A form like a Luna moth flitted toward her, its voice high and sweet as it whispered, "You are returned to free us as you did so long ago."

She recognized this spirit from Ariel's magical feast and remembered what those spirits had said, as she realized, "You were trapped?" The moth flitted up and down as if nodding.

"Yes, and then we vanished you." This voice was lower, belonging to a robin-like spirit.

"We saved you from this place as you saved us from her." It was the moth again. Her voice was familiar, somehow.

A starling added, "And we sent you to seek Leana the raven in the Canyon. To ask for her aid."

"To escape from *her*."

"To escape the summoner."

Until this moment, Alda had assumed that either the witches or the bubble had taken her to the Canyon. She broke the spirits' brisk chatter. "What did Sycorax do?"

"She stole us."

"Used us."

"Took our sisters and mothers and cousins."

"She built us into her walls and palaces."

"Used us as material."

"I don't understand." Alda knew enough of Netherfeld's magic to glean that one could create with her mind. That she could imagine something and then make it real, somehow, simply by being in this realm. So why did Sycorax need to use the spirits?

"Her own magic dwindled." Again, the moth's words ran smoothly together. "The magic within her was like a dry well so she needed to use another source and she chose us."

The robin interjected, "She chose to use us like so many bricks."

"And I allowed her to do this?" Alda felt a knot in her stomach rise to her throat. These spirits were creatures, sentient, not to be forced into some act against their will.

"You did not know until we told you."

"And then you helped us stop her."

Alda understood. "You helped me build the prison?

Rather, you were the prison. To protect the other spirits. And you helped protect me as well."

Again, the green Luna moth flitted an affirmation. "She tried to attack and destroy you but we would not let her."

"Why would you save me?"

The moth hovered near Alda's face, its luminous wings obscuring the other spirits who continued to swirl and bend in the air around them as it whispered, "Because I am your mother of course."

Alda gasped, and her voice cracked in disbelief, "Phillida? Is it truly you?"

The moth flitted above, as if startled by a sudden blast of wind. The other spirits followed her, swirling up into the sky like some ominous cloud. Green light flashed in the distance. Again, brighter. Or closer.

"Quiet! It is coming. We must go to the floating waters." The robin's words were high. Urgent.

Despite herself, Alda felt her jaw clench with fear. "What is coming?"

"Danger."

The spirits swirled away like leaves on a brisk breeze, but Alda hesitated in the darkness. The spirits, in the past, were her allies. Should she trust them, now? Could she believe them?

But there was no alternative. Nothing else, no one else, to help her find her way in the endless, empty realm.

So Alda followed as best she could, trotting beneath and behind the spirits. She asked with unsteady words, "What are the floating waters?"

The hovering spirits remained silent as they led her through the vast expanse of Netherfeld's darkness.

*   *   *

As they walked through the darkness of Netherfeld, Dreng told his tale in quick whispers, relaying the events at the cottage to Caliban as they approached a crumbling, dilapidated tower. "And the flood, it, it separated us..."

His voice was lost as he saw that the lonely tower was not crumbling. Its form was gray in parts, invisible. Like a painting with a chipped surface. Or chalk letters washed away by water.

Caliban entered through a stone archway at the base of the tower, and Dreng reluctantly followed. The doorway led to a small corridor with a spiral stairway that ascended into blackness above.

Dreng stopped and stared. "What is this place?"

"My chateau." Caliban smiled, and Dreng could not tell if it was pride or sarcasm that penetrated his tone. "I created it."

"Why?"

"I needed a place to hide bodies." He motioned to the stairs, as if they held some sinister secret.

But Dreng understood his sarcasm. "You live here now?"

Caliban scoffed, "This is something less than living." As Caliban spoke, the archway filled with mossy stones as pieces of stairway vanished before them.

Dreng stared, amazed.

"But this place is sturdy enough. And safe." Caliban held out a hand expectantly, and Dreng returned the cloak to him.

As Caliban tied it over his shoulders, he stepped on the first stair and touched a faded stone. It became solid at his fingertips. He turned back to Dreng and studied his eyes. "You look like you've seen a ghost."

"I have." As soon as Dreng spoke, he regretted revealing this secret.

Caliban laughed. Dreng did not.

Caliban's eyes brimmed with curiosity as he descended the step. "A ghost? What kind?"

Dreng remembered it on the island, outside Alda's cottage. In the curtain of rain. The bearded spectre, its skin glowing yet transparent. It was a spectacle of horror. Not real, not human. But Dreng could not describe it thus, so he shrugged and avoided Caliban's gaze. "My father."

"When?"

"On several occasions."

"What did it say?"

"When?" Dreng skirted the question and wished he could take back his words, but he remembered its warning. Its command to kill the witch that had taken his life.

"On those several occasions."

Dreng sighed, "I don't remember."

"Speak the truth."

"It's insignificant. Worthless."

"It is not." Caliban stepped forward boldly, gripping tightly to his sword. "Tell me what the ghost said, when you most recently conversed with it."

"My name."

"Is that all?"

"No."

Caliban crossed his arms and feigned anger. "What else?"

Dreng clenched his fists and looked for some escape, some way to turn their discussion. But he was trapped. "He said that in order to stop the witches, I had to give them what they wanted."

"Which is?"

"I don't know."

"You don't?"

"No." But Dreng now suspected that they wanted *him*.

"How do you know that ghost, as you call it, was truly your father?"

Dreng shook his head. He had no answer.

"Did you test it? Ask a question only he would know?"

"Yes, I asked the spectre for my name."

"But how would you know if what it spoke was true?"

Dreng met Caliban with silence, so the beautiful youth continued, "Did you ever doubt its words?"

Doubt. The word brought him back to Miranda — no, Sycorax — before the cavern crumbled, and the anger he felt then rose back into his voice as he hissed through gritted teeth, "I may not have known my father. But I know who *I* am. And I can still recognize truth."

Even as he said it, he knew it to be a lie. His wife, her false identity, proved it so.

Caliban laughed again and held his haughty chin aloft as he met Dreng's stare. "What is truth, boy?"

"Don't call me that."

"It is what he called you, isn't it? Your Danish prince?"

Dreng avoided his eyes. Caliban was right — the word *dreng* meant boy — so he quickly changed the subject. "What are you doing in Netherfeld?"

"Searching."

"For what?"

"Truth."

"And what is truth, oh great seer?" Dreng's sarcasm weighed on the final word.

"Truth is the backside of falsehood." Caliban made a movement to indicate another meaning of "backside."

Dreng did his best to suppress a snicker. "You cannot define a concept by what it is not."

"Then you define it."

Dreng considered. "Truth is the end of reckoning."

"That's a start."

Dreng scowled, "How could you determine truth, if you do not know what is false?"

"There's the rub."

"The what?"

"Dilemma." Caliban wiped his fingers over his chin and sneered, "Tell me, where is your wife?"

"Trapped in a frozen spring." Dreng answered without hesitation. But he suspected there was more to it than that.

Caliban raised his eyebrows. "Do you want to save her?"

Dreng drew a deep breath and exhaled slowly. "Yes." He immediately regretted his response. Finding Alda was more important.

"Then help me discover what is true."

"What do you mean?"

Caliban turned abruptly and walked away from the stairs to an empty area of the small room. "Come with me."

"Where?"

"To meet someone."

"Who?"

Dreng could hear the smile behind Caliban's words. "No one."

As Dreng watched, mouth agape, Caliban waved his hand, and the stones at their feet disappeared. A new set of stairs appeared, straight and narrow, that became obscured by darkness some distance below the ground.

"Once more into the breach!" Caliban stepped lightly down the stairs, and Dreng hesitantly followed. The walls became more ruinous as they descended, parts entirely obscured in blackness and others transparent. Soon, Dreng had the sensation that they were deep below ground. If such a realm had a ground.

Finally, the beautiful youth reached the final step and entered a windowless corridor, his pace quickening. Dreng forced his weakened limbs to match his companion's steps as he panted, "Where are we going?"

He half expected some sarcastic response, a reference to death or such, but Caliban was serious. "To interrogate my prisoner."

"Prisoner? Who?"

"Time will tell."

Chapter Five: False of Heart

As Alda continued to follow the spirits in the unbroken nothing of Netherfeld, she could no longer hold her tongue. So she trotted closer to the moth and whispered, "Are you truly Phillida?"

It cooed only, "Yes."

"But, how did you get here?" Alda needed a way to test it, so she lied, "In Fairy Land, I saw you pass through a circle of flowers. What happened after that?"

The moth stopped its wings and glided for a moment before it replied. "I did not enter the flowered circle child, you helped me into the door in the tree."

Alda was satisfied. "Of course. Where did the door lead?"

"To a land of flowers."

"Flowers?"

"Yes fennel and columbine... daisies... violets... all so lovely."

"And then what happened?" Alda realized her pace had slowed, so she ran faster to not fall behind the other spirits.

"The witches found me there and wanted me to join them because I am descended from Hecate... but I did not." It fluttered anxiously. "The witches destroyed my body and sent me here with no form" The moth paused.

"But over time I repaired myself and became a Luna."

"But I met you before, as a moth, on Prospero's island. Why did you not speak to me then, tell me who you were?" She paused and corrected, "Are."

"It was not time my child."

Alda studied the other forms, swirling above. Some were only lights like ribbon, flitting through the darkness, some geometric shapes like cubes or pyramids. Others were animals a-flight, their glowing wings cutting through the dark. "Were these all people, once?"

"Some were and others have only existed in spirit form."

"Who were they?"

"We do not speak to one another of the past, my child, because that is not where we are." The moth moved to Alda's other side and flew higher than the others. "We see what is before us and with us now and hold blinders over what has been because that is not where we want to be."

"And what is the danger you fear now? Is it the witches?"

Again, the moth stopped beating its wings and coasted gracefully through the air. When it reached Alda's knees, it flapped urgently and lifted to the height of her face. "They are close."

Alda felt a lump form in her throat as she asked

again, "What is the floating water?"

She was met with silence. So she followed obediently, her thoughts bending to Fairy Land and her discovery of her lost mother in that enchanted forest. Broken and confined. Lacking will and empathy. And love. She was cold and, worse, deceptive.

Alda knew that Phillida was not a mother, not truly, which is why she did not mourn her injury in Oberon's court or her passing through the many-doored tree into an unknown realm. She was like a stranger, a character in a book of fantastical tales. Still, Alda knew that she should love her mother. But she could not.

Yet she was grateful for some connection, no matter how distant, in this place of nothing.

Although she would have preferred to find Dreng. Or her grandmother.

"Where is Gramma?" Alda had not intended to speak the words aloud, but they escaped from her lips along with her thought.

The moth sped farther ahead, so Alda quickened her pace to remain
below it as she persisted, "I have seen her here before. Where is she now?"

Several moments passed in silence before the moth whispered, "She is weak."

"Why? What happened?" Fear raised the pitch of

Alda's voice.

"She tried to hold them at bay."

"Tried? Did she fail?"

Again, silence.

"Phillida, tell me what happened!" The sudden exclamation felt like a knot in Alda's throat. She pressed her hand against a cramp in her side and gasped for breath, suddenly winded. For a moment, she thought she could not take another step.

"We are here." The robin's timely words quelled Alda's worries. Or rather, redirected them. Above the spirits, some distance above Alda's head, was a swirling torrent. It looked like the Grand River after the spring frost: foamy waves lapping and dancing, splashes sending droplets into the air. Blue light shown through, reflecting on its glistening surface.

But the water was above them all, perfectly suspended, its edges fading into the surrounding darkness. Like a distant galaxy on a moonless night. Alda reached above her head, trying to touch its glistening surface, but it was too far.

"You cannot reach it." The voice echoed through the nothing, sending some spirits scattering up and out.

It was human. Soft and light. A girl.

"Sycorax?" Alda held her breath, fearing the summoner might have returned too soon.

"No." The unseen girl laughed, high and jovial. "She is dead, of course. My father killed her. And even if she somehow survived, she would be old and crooked by now."

Why did the girl not reveal herself? What was she hiding? *Why* was she hiding? "Who are you?"

"Yes! I *do* know you. You are the strange person from the beach, the girl to whom I gave my cloak." Her tone darkened. "I should have kept my cloak, I suppose. I might not be here if I had kept it."

"Miranda?"

The voice laughed, high and innocent. "Who else? You and I are the only girls ever to be on Father's island."

The spirits stopped their frantic whirling and hovered once more in the air, their light illuminating the darkness below the floating water.

Yet Miranda was still hidden. "Where are you?"

"Here!"

"Where?"

"I am standing next to you, friend."

Alda turned and looked to all sides. "I cannot see you."

"Nor can I see myself. Here, let me show you my hand. Look up!" Above her head, Alda saw a silhouette of long fingers and a narrow palm, its form like a shadow against the blue waters above.

Unlike the walking shadows Alda had encountered earlier in Netherfeld — the forms of those born from

Ophelia's imagination — this figure was black, like all around it.

"Why are you invisible?"

"Invisible? Yes, I suppose I am. I thought it was more like a trick of concealment, as seahorses hide in ocean greens. This is how I have always been, since I have been in this place."

"How did you get here?"

"Oh, that is such a story! I was bored for so long that I finally summoned the courage to find my Cali, and I took my cloak for protection."

"Cali?" The spirits swirled excitedly at the name, streaking past Alda's head.

"Caliban! You must certainly know him! He is the only boy on Father's island."

Alda nodded, suppressing questions.

"And then I saw you on the beach, and I was so close to Cali's home in the cave, and I thought I could surely get there before Father's spirits came for the horrible men from the ship. So I gave you my cloak. But I was too slow. And the spirits were too fast. So they took me here."

"You are dead." Alda intended to speak questioningly, but her tone dropped too much on the final word.

"Oh, no! Father would never kill anyone. He is far too kind."

Alda felt her brow furrow. Moments before, this girl

had said her father had killed Sycorax.

But Miranda continued, unaware of her mistake. "No, his spell simply separates a person's being from his body."

Alda bit her lip and did her best to look squarely at the voice's source. "Is that not death?" The spirits around them once again swirled, their forms flitting beneath the water above.

"Of course not! For the being only comes here to wait for a reunion with its flesh."

"You are in limbo, then." Alda shivered. The girl's light mood was unnerving.

"I am awaiting my return to my body, yes."

Alda knew that Miranda's body was already in use. Sycorax had taken it. "And what if you cannot return to your body?"

"Oh, I will not return by myself. My father will find me and restore me."

"How?"

"He is ever so clever, my father, Prospero. He will send his harpy to find me and make me whole again."

"But what if he —" Alda paused, worry pressing her brow. "Cannot?"

"Then I will have to wait longer, I suppose." An awkward silence. "But I am patient."

And Alda realized she had another question: "Why

were you going to Caliban's cave?"

"To see him and to play games." Her words were innocent, as if the answer was universally understood. She frowned. "I told you, I was bored."

"Did you plan to run away together, or —"

"Oh, no. Cali did not know I was coming. Years have passed since I last visited him. It was a surprise. He loves surprises."

Alda suppressed a snicker.

Miranda did not seem to notice and continued, "And Father had kept me away for so very long. But I am older now, old enough to make my own decisions. And I told Father such earlier, but he would not listen to me. So I snuck out when he was busy with the invading ship and went to see my Cali and tell him that I love him still, despite —" She paused, her breath audible as she searched for the proper word. "Despite his unfortunate appearance."

Again, Miranda paused, her breathing fast and heavy in the void. "And now that you are here with me, my friend, you can help me return to him."

"How?"

"The waters above are part of an enchanted stream that leads to Father's island. My father told me stories of it, warned me not to go near it. It is like a tunnel between this world and mine. So I can use it to return. Just hoist me up to touch it, and then I can go home."

"But what of me?" Alda's tone shook with worry.

"Yes, I suppose you should come along as well. Can your lights lift you up once I have passed through? Can you command them to do your bidding as Father commands his to do his unwanted labor?"

Alda looked to the spirits, her eyes filled with unspoken questions.

"We will help." The melodious voice of the robin whispered in Alda's ear. Its words grew softer so only Alda could hear. "But this girl is dangerous."

Chapter Six: All the Devils

Dreng descended into the depths beneath Caliban's tower, following the beautiful youth into the darkness below. He expected some odor, some smell of tepid water and rot. But this place, the realm of Netherfeld, had no such scent. Rather, it had no scent whatsoever, no discerning features apart from the grim tower, its underground labyrinth, and its vanishing form.

Twenty paces. Fifty. The ceiling lowered, and Dreng had to bow his head as he stayed on Caliban's heels, the position reminding him of being in the hold of *The Tempest*. Ten more steps, and they reached a small, solid, metal door in the floor. Etched into its surface was a spiral, matching the one on the floor of the library in Prospero's palace.

And near the door was a simple, wooden lever.

"What is this place?"

Caliban stooped and moved his cloak aside as he placed his hand against the lever. "An *oubliette*. A place to forget. But we must remember. And find truth." He smiled and added, "And wisdom." The beautiful youth pulled, and the door fell open with a rusty squeal.

Dreng leaned over the small opening, his eyes unable to adjusted to the darkness within. "What's ins—" Before Dreng could utter the final syllable, he felt himself hit a stone floor, his shoulder crumbling beneath the weight of his body.

For a moment, Dreng lay as he had fallen, confused and stunned. The darkness enveloped him, like in the cavern, except for the opening some ten feet above his head. It closed with a screech, and he heard a latch as the remnants of light danced behind his eyelids.

His vision adjusted, and the phantom lights ceased as he considered what to do.

He could call out. For help. For Caliban. But this was his doing, some game, some trick. And Dreng doubted there was danger, not real and immediate danger, yet his heart pounded against his ears.

And his shoulder throbbed. It was out of joint, bent strangely forward above his tingling arm and useless fingers. This was not the first time it had been injured thus, so he held his breath and clenched his jaw as he twisted and popped it back into position.

Only a slight hiccup of pain escaped his lips.

He wiped the fresh sweat from his forehead and tried to reason through Caliban's words: "A place to forget, but we must remember, and find truth and wisdom."

But he had mentioned a prisoner. *Prisoner*.

The word stuck in his mind as Dreng realized that he might be Caliban's prey. Perhaps this was indeed a trap, not a trick.

Perhaps Dreng was the prisoner.

But, if the witches had spoken truth, it was not Dreng's time to die. There was no singing mountain, no fire. If Dreng had more confidence, more optimism, he might even think himself invincible because surely stones could not sing or burn. But he had seen so much since he had arrived on Prospero's island.

And before that, Dreng had survived worse.

Years earlier, after Prince Hamlet had escaped, when the young ship-boy had been bandaged and his wound from Ernesto began to show its first signs of improvement, he was suddenly thrown into the dank hold and bound to a munitions barrel, his shoulders twisted behind him and his wrists searing against rough rope. He struggled to stand but could not brace his feet against the slick planks. So he sat in the damp and listened to the scurry of rats, waiting for what punishment would come.

After what felt like days, a hooded figure appeared. Dreng expected execution, but he instead got a bloodied nose and aching jaw. The boy pleaded and begged and cried and offered to tell the man anything, to do anything, to make the beating stop. Only silence met him and then, again, Dreng was alone. The next day was the same. And the next and the next until his every breath rattled with pain and hunger and thirst and his pleas that sounded so empty as they echoed against the wooden beams.

Finally, Dreng stopped speaking. He took the punches and kicks and worse.

And then, suddenly, they stopped.

One night, after passing out from exhaustion and agony, he awoke to find the ropes gone. Stale bread and flat ale had been placed on the barrel. He ate and drank and, after settling his nerves, snuck to the deck above and slumbered in relative peace on his old coiled rope.

The next morning, as the sun rose, he reunited with the crew.

He counted their number. It measured the same as his beatings. Each had his revenge firsthand.

And no one ever spoke of what transpired in the hold, not even on the day of his trial by sword.

But Dreng had learned the importance of revenge and silence. And he was also taught to be hard, to outlast the men who caused pain and fear, to guard himself against what danger might come.

To survive.

As Dreng's mind returned to his immediate predicament, he shuddered and rose unsteadily to his feet, outstretched his arms, and took tentative steps into the darkness.

Four paces ahead, and his fingers touched a wall. Two to the left, and another wall. He turned around, toward the direction that had been his right, and his third step landed on something soft.

He knelt and felt a jumble of rags. Skin, warm. Long hair, coarse. A beard. Breath. He gently shook the figure, but it did not stir.

Should he speak?

Should he cry out for aid, for Caliban?

No, this was Caliban's aim. This, the prisoner. So Dreng leaned closer to the inanimate man and whispered, "I can help you."

Silence. So Dreng continued, "Tell me who you are."

A deep breath, held, and released with a sigh and a cough.

Dreng felt his companion move and steadied his shaking form as he tried to sit. Finally, after the man could sit unaided, he responded hoarsely, "I am Prospero."

The name was unexpected here, in the prison of forgetfulness. The man who had destroyed *The Tempest* and killed Dreng's crewmates. A murderer and a tyrant.

Prospero was dead. Miranda — no, Sycorax — had told Dreng so. He had died in the library, somehow, and the only trace of his struggle was a spiral on the floor.

The same spiral that adorned the trapdoor above.

So Sycorax had lied. The old man, the one who commanded spirits and controlled the enchanted island, lived but had been transported to another realm.

For a brief flash, Dreng wondered if she had spoken

truth. Perhaps this was death, the world beyond. Perhaps, as he had feared, the flood had indeed washed him and Alda not to another realm but to a watery grave.

But no. Sycorax had lied, and this was real. Dreng could feel his existence, even now. He was yet alive.

And so was Prospero.

After the shock had subsided, Dreng asked quietly, "How did you get here?"

"Who are you?"

The question caught Dreng off guard. He had two names now and had to choose. "My name is Thomas Chatterton." The words immediately felt foreign. The title of a stranger.

And he was met with silence again.

So Dreng continued, "I can help you, if you tell me how you got here."

Again, the old man did not respond. So Dreng persisted, "What does Caliban want with you?"

"How would I know the wants of a monster?"

Dreng felt his fingers curl into a fist, and it took all his resolve to hold his temper at bay. "*You* are the monster."

The sorcerer laughed, the sound quickly becoming a cough.

"You are three steps behind him, boy. Caliban will destroy you, as he has ruined me."

A sly smile spread across Dreng's lips, unseen in the

darkness as he lied, "Yes, I know. Certainly. How can we defeat him?"

"With wisdom."

"What kind of wisdom?"

The old man shifted away, and a chill rose up Dreng's neck as silence once more permeated the black chamber.

And, finally, the old man spoke...

After some minutes of repeated questioning, Dreng shouted for Caliban's help and begged for their release from the *oubliette*. But Dreng could hear the reluctance in his captor's reply as he refused to lift him to safety.

Finally, Dreng lied and told the beautiful youth that Prospero had revealed the secret wisdom.

Caliban was still suspicious, his tone clear even as his words were lost in echoes, and it was not until Dreng swore an oath not to retaliate that a rope hit the stony floor in the darkness, and Dreng pushed the old man up to safety and then awkwardly heaved his own weight into the tower's underground corridor, wincing in pain from his too-recent injuries.

In the relative light above the cell, Dreng could examine his fellow prisoner for the first time. He had not seen Prospero previously but had heard enough from Miranda — Sycorax — to paint a picture in his mind.

This man before him was not what he had anticipated. His emaciated form was shrouded in a thick robe. His face obscured by a beard. His hair gray and thinning. The man's eyes were cast downward, ignoring those near him. He was weak. Frightened.

Dreng looked from him to Caliban, his eyes full of questions.

With a snort, Caliban spat, "You two have not had the pleasure of a formal introduction. This specimen was until recently Dreng, the once and future Thomas Chatterton, former pirate and current — I don't know what."

"Yes, I already —"

Caliban paid Dreng no regard. "And this abomination, miscreant, stock-fish, this, this spongy mushrump is Prospero, father of Miranda, former sorcerer, usurper, and then destroyer of my hopes and dreams." The young man spat.

Prospero cast a wicked look at Dreng, who stood and looked down at the man's ragged form. One who had once controlled unknown powers now looked only sad. An old man to be pitied, not feared.

"Did he give it to you?" Caliban glanced at Dreng, and his eyes appeared more mournful than his tone revealed. "He refuses to even speak a word to me. And if he speaks, I expect only lies."

"Why should I tell you what he said?" For once, Dreng was a step ahead of Caliban, and he did not attempt to hide the victorious sneer on his face.

"I saved your life. I protected you from the witches."
Caliban leaned toward him, slowing to enunciate each
word with the full weight of his threat. "And if you do not
help me now, I will make certain that they find you again.
And then there will be no *deus ex machina* to save you."

Dreng laughed, despite the shiver that tickled his
neck. This was not the boy on the raft, not the same
sarcastic witticisms or insolent sneers. This was
something dark; some madness had overtaken the
beautiful youth. And where would that madness lead? To
Dreng's death, or his own?

Or both?

But Dreng suppressed his worries and focused with
the steadiness of character that he commanded as
boatswain, his voice unwavering as he spoke to Caliban.
"How long have you held him here?"

"This place has no days or months or years. There is
no moon or sun. No seasons, so —"

"How long?"

"More than long enough for him to give me what I
want."

Dreng crouched by the old man's side and reached
for his bearded face, which turned away not in fear but in
some kind of haughty pride. After a moment, Dreng stood
and sighed, "He told me that he has the wisdom you seek

but would not share it with you or anyone." Dreng set his
jaw and added, "So we must kill him."

Even Caliban gasped, but Dreng did not flinch. He
had seen this resolution before. In himself.

And now, above the *oubliette*, Dreng saw a familiar,
steely look in Prospero's eyes as he stood above the
captive. So Dreng repeated to Caliban, "Kill him."

Chapter Seven: Deepest Consequences

Below the glistening, floating waters, Alda felt an unsettling sense of urgency as the spirits swirled around her, their forms brushing against her arms and skirt, their lights unnaturally bright in the surrounding nothing of Netherfeld.

And Alda did not attempt to suppress her smile as Miranda's empty silhouette again broke the silence. "If we are to leave this place, then I must bid it farewell properly."

The girl was so innocent, so sweet and kind. Sincere and pure. Strangely, she was the opposite of Caliban. Perhaps the cliché about loving opposites was true after all.

Or perhaps what they had together was not love. Only some trick. Like Dreng's enchantment.

But Alda shook her head. Surely there was good in the world, and this girl was of it.

"Goodbye, my dear spirits." The forms of light spun wildly like bees kicked from a hive as Miranda spoke.

Alda stepped back, growing worry weighing on her brow.

The innocent girl continued, "Goodbye, sweet, black nothing."

Some spirits flashed, their lights sparking into the blackness.

The moth form of Phillida glided closer to Alda, the

only calm spirit in the pandemonium. "Alda my dear," she whispered. "You must prepare yourself."

Before Alda could respond, Miranda continued, "Farewell, my newfound friends!"

Lightning. Again. A third flash connected a few yards from Alda, the light dazzling her eyes to near blindness. And when she opened them, she saw three familiar figures.

Witches.

"All hail, Alda!" The voice was hoarse, its words sarcastic.

"Hail, heir of Hecate!"

"Hail, the living girl."

"Who will die."

Alda backed away from the weird sisters, positioning herself beneath the Stream of Consciousness. She could feel the spirits swirling above and behind her but dared not turn her head toward them as she retorted, "We will all die someday."

"She sees the truth, sister."

"Too little, though."

"And too late."

"The rest she'll know in the grave."

"Let's not speak of such morbid things!" Miranda's enthusiastic voice broke though the whirring spirits. "Friends, do you already know one another?"

The witches laughed as Alda pleaded, "Miranda, come with me!" She could not leave Miranda with them as she had abandoned Ophelia.

But what might happen to the girl without a body on the other side of the stream?

Surely she would be a shade, as Sycorax had been. But Alda could protect her there, on the island. Then she could find Dreng, somehow. And together, with the cauldron's bubble, they could find Caliban. And —

Alda's hopes were interrupted as she realized she was suddenly suspended, lifted toward the Stream of Consciousness by the spirits.

Again, she tried, "Miranda, these beings are dangerous! Do not remain here!"

But Miranda laughed, and the sound revealed that the formless voice had moved closer to the three witches.

"But these are *my* friends. They found me here. And helped guide me to this stream. And then they told me to wait — here — and that an enemy would soon come."

"Enemy?"

"You." Four voices spoke in unison.

Miranda laughed, and Alda realized that her innocence was a ploy. This girl was clever. And the spirits were correct: she was dangerous.

So Alda reached for the stream, her fingertips only inches from its enchanted waters. But then she fell. Not

completely to the ground, but near enough. She wiped
her hair from her eyes and saw plumes of smoke
dissipate above her head. Yet she was suspended by the
spirits, despite their dwindled numbers.

She realized that the spirits were the smoke. The
witches had destroyed them.

And a cold grip encircled Alda's ankle as some
unseen force pulled her down, toward the witches.

Before Alda could react, the robin and starling and
several formless swirls dove at the witches, who with a
wave turned them to pillars of smoke that quickly
dissolved. As if they had never existed.

But whatever encircled her ankle loosed its grip as the
five spirits that still hoisted Alda aloft lifted her closer to the
stream. The Luna moth flew at her side, its voice shaking as
it gasped, "Only a little farther my dear and you will be safe…
but you must not forget me when you are gone."

"No! Let me stay and fight!" Alda struggled and
dropped again, but the spirits held firm and moved faster
toward the stream. Three spirits let loose and again charged
the witches, only to be instantaneously dissolved as well.

Each time the witches waved their hands, they
cackled. Miranda joined in their mirth, her laugh more
shrill than the others. "Yes, yes, let her stay!"

Alda could not determine if the girl found joy in the
spirits' destruction or was unaware of the witches'

wickedness. She shivered.

Now, Alda ascended slower as only a sparrow and the Luna moth remained at her side, hoisting her arms toward the underside of the water. She reached, and her fingers felt its droplets.

As she was thrust into the stream's depths, Alda's last thought was of her mother, trapped in Netherfeld with the witches. But Phillida had escaped worse, surely. She was strong enough to survive the witches' wrath.

And suddenly, Alda was elsewhere. Her worries distant and overpowered.

She knew it was a dream — no, a memory — but that did not make it easier to overcome. Although she was within the depths of the Stream of Consciousness, she had no sensation of its waters.

Instead, she was a little girl again on the seventh island in the cottage, looking at stereopticon cards as her grandmother kneaded bread on the large wooden table.

"Tell me a story, Gramma."

"No, I want to hear *your* story."

Little Alda lowered her stereoscope and gave her grandmother a serious look, one that felt too mature for her age. "I don't have any. I'm not old enough."

"Nonsense! You have your stories there, in your hand. Tell me about them."

"These are only pictures."

"Then give them words."

Alda hesitated and sorted through her cards. Her favorites were of
the flora and fauna of distant lands, watercolored images of Australian marsupials and South American jungles. She selected one of a reef and placed it carefully on the wire rack. As she looked at its image, the corals seemingly so close that she might touch them, she whispered, "There was a mermaid who lived in an enchanted reef, a young mermaid. A girl, like me. And she found a fish trapped under a pirate ship's anchor, so she freed it."

"Go on."

"But it wasn't an ordinary fish. It was the color of amethyst, and it could talk. So when the mermaid freed it, it gave her three wishes."

"And what did she wish for?"

Alda lowered the stereoscope and bit her lip. "She wished to see the world." She sorted through other cards, grasping for inspiration. "She wished for knowledge, more knowledge than she could get beneath the sea. And..." Her voice trailed off as she watched her grandmother turn and pound the dough. "And she wished to find her family."

"Well, the mermaid should know that she can see the world without help from a magical fish." She smiled slyly. "And that she can find her own knowledge."

"But family —"

"Family, too." Gramma stopped kneading long enough to smile at Alda and wiped a floury hand across her forehead. "You can choose those you are with, those whom you love. Or you can choose to be alone." Her eyes narrowed as her gaze became more intense. "Remember this, Alda. But now, be like your mermaid. Swim!"

And Alda became aware of her legs and her arms, flailing in the stream. She imagined its smooth surface, the flowering dryads above, and she kicked and pulled and finally gulped the island's air.

But then she fell into another memory, one more recent. In her cottage with Dreng, delirious from his poisoned wound. Sweat dripping from his forehead, his shoulders shaking and breath heaving from his chest. She wiped his hair from his face with a cold cloth, and his eyes opened for a flash before turning upward, their spheres only white.

His lips moved, urgently, but no sound escaped.

Suddenly, his mouth opened in a silent scream, and then he was still. Too still. And for a moment Alda was on edge. No movement. So she felt his chest. Nothing. No heartbeat, no breath.

Alda gasped and choked on a sob, and for a flash her eyes focused on the present, on the stream's shoreline. She pulled again, knowing that Dreng was only a horrible dream. That the shore was real. That she had to reach it.

That she had to save herself.

But she fell into her memory again, and her cheeks were wet with tears. She held her wrist over Dreng's lips, feeling for air. Nothing. She held her shaking finger to his neck, as her grandmother had taught her to do, and waited in the deafening silence.

Finally, Alda felt her hand close on a root, and she dragged her body from the enchanted waters.

She was on the island, again.

But as she coughed and choked and finally smiled at her successful escape, her mind was still with Dreng.

She thought he had died then. For a terrible moment, she feared he had left her alone in the cottage. But she had felt a distant echo of his heartbeat. And then his breaths returned, steady. His fever broke, the poison somehow sweated from his quivering form. And as he slept on her tapestried sofa, she cried over him. Tears of relief and sadness and fear and uncertainty.

And now, on the bank of the Stream of Consciousness, she felt tears again flood her eyes. But she quickly brushed them away.

He was alive, somewhere, she reminded herself. She had saved him in her cottage.

As the fear from her memory faded, Alda had only one desire: to save him again.

But first she had to find him.

Chapter Eight: Mischiefs Manifold

As they stood in the vanishing tower's depths, the corridor's ceiling weighing down on them, Dreng tried to make himself look larger than he felt. Intimidating.

Prospero remained defiantly silent, scowling, so Dreng continued, "In the *oubliette*, he told me that he has a pearl of wisdom, some secret of knowledge, but that he could not share it."

"Why not?"

"He said that we are too simple to use it."

Caliban laughed. "We? Us? Too simple? I? I am the heir to a great kingdom. And you, the — well, you are still alive, so surely that is significant."

"Caliban, it is a trick." Dreng enunciated each word slowly as he wiped his hand across his brow. "That is why we must kill him."

"But then we will never find the pearl of wisdom!" Dreng disregarded Caliban's protest and took hold of the sword at his companion's waist as Caliban objected, "No, no, not yet. What if, what if..." His words faded into the depths of the corridor.

"Why do you hesitate?"

Caliban mumbled, "Conscience makes me a coward."

"I have no such reservation!" Dreng held the sword aloft, its blade pointed at Prospero's throat. But Caliban pushed the weapon aside and stood between them as the old man cowered on the stony floor of the disintegrating tower.

"Do I want him dead? Surely. But not enough to kill him. Let him suffer instead. Let him wither. Let him be forgotten. But do not kill him, Dreng. Death is too kind."

A wail echoed through the dim light. Not a scream of pain. A sob.
Dreng smiled and lowered the blade as Caliban crouched beside the old
man.

"You would let me live, boy?"

"Only as you let me live. A miserable outcast, torn from —" Caliban stood as he added, "I loved your daughter once. And still, despite myself. That makes you somewhat more like kin. Though less than kind."

The old man broke down into a wretched pile of tears and wails, so Dreng dropped the sword to his side as he turned to Caliban. "If you won't let me kill him, then what shall we do?"

"You and I can return to the island. *My* island. There is enough knowledge in the library to help us stop the witches." He took a deep breath as he replaced the sword on his waist. "I hope."

"Take me with you!" Prospero's voice cracked as he pleaded. "I will be at your service. You will command my obedience. I swear to you, I swear to you on —"

"On my mother's grave?" Caliban's voice shook with fury. He again bent to the old man and studied his face. "Usurper, if you want to be free, tell me where to find the damned pearl."

Confusion flashed over Dreng's face. Did Caliban want a pearl? A *literal* pearl of wisdom?

Prospero shook his head, so Caliban grabbed him roughly by the front of his shirt. "My mother and I tore apart your staff when we sent you to this wretched place! It was in splinters, but its magic was gone. Disappeared. The seed that let its power grow was nowhere to be found." He spoke through clenched teeth. "Where did you hide the blasted pearl of wisdom?"

The old sorcerer coughed and turned his head away silently. The young man relented, a look not of anger but of profound disappointment crossing his face. "My friend was going to kill you, Prospero. He is mad. But I stopped him. I let you live. And still, you will not surrender the one token that I need to free your daughter from an icy grave."

Dreng turned, concealing the look of surprise on his face. Caliban knew that the grave held Sycorax, not Miranda, so this was a purposeful lie. Dreng could not let his unchecked expression betray whatever his companion was planning.

"Let me save her, Prospero!" His voice cracked. "The

pearl. Now."

"You are like the devil, Caliban. Spinning a web of deceit and ensnaring those around you."

"You confuse me with a spider. Harmless if left to my own devices."

The old man scowled and coughed again, the sound deep and worrisome. He raised himself up on one elbow and reached his free hand into his mouth. His face twisted in pain and effort until he produced in his palm a single, white tooth.

But Dreng could see it was no tooth. Its shape too round, its surface too smooth. It was a pearl.

Prospero thrust it into Caliban's hand as he proclaimed, "Here is the pearl of wisdom. Now let me go free!"

Caliban smiled at the tiny jewel and placed it within the fabric at his waist. His expression changed suddenly as he looked back at the old man. "Free you? I said that I would let you be forgotten." He lunged forward and pushed Prospero back through the open door of the *oubliette*. A deep thud echoed from below before Caliban dropped the metal door with a reverberating clank.

"You will leave him here to die?" Dreng's words shook.

"One cannot die from hunger or thirst in Netherfeld. He will survive." He paused and added, "But what is it to you? You were going to kill him."

"I told you it was a trick."

Caliban smiled slyly. "And I played my part as well. Are we offstage now?"

Dreng nodded reluctantly. All was deception with Caliban. Well, most. So he doubted that he would receive a clear answer, yet he asked, "What is the pearl of wisdom?"

Caliban, to his surprise, was earnest. "It is like a prism that magnifies the sun. But this jewel intensifies magic. Any spell, any power, is amplified by its touch."

"Then it can find Alda."

Caliban cleared his throat, the sound unnaturally loud in the empty corridor. "In time, friend. First, we must awaken my mother. Your *wife*." The word felt cruel, like a dagger.

The beautiful youth turned and started down the corridor, and Dreng shivered as the cries of the prisoner echoed hollowly beneath him.

*   *   *

The island was not as Alda had remembered. The sun's orb was still as bright and the sky was the same shade of azure blue, but the sounds and the colors were all muted. No, not muted. Absent.

Flowers. Leaves. Life. All gone.

No naiads emerged, sparkling and misty, from the enchanted waters of the Stream of Consciousness. The dryads — oaken nymphs — no longer dipped and swayed above the streambank. They stood white and barren, like an elephant graveyard in one of Alda's stereopticon cards. White. Sun-scorched. Dead.

Alda shivered. How much time had passed on Prospero's island? Had she arrived at some distant point in the future, after years or decades or centuries had done their work?

Or had something horrible happened?

Another shiver. Alda wrung the dripping water from her black hair and gray skirt and hesitated longer than she should before she approached the naked trunk of a deceased dryad.

For a moment, Alda recalled a moment from her childhood. When she was younger and happier, she was tasked with trapping a wild squirrel that ravaged her grandmother's herb garden. So she rigged a trap from broken planks and frayed rope and waited patiently for her target to creep beneath its wooden prison. The squirrel finally came, and she captured it with ease.

But then she discovered that the squirrel was injured, its foot bleeding from the weight of the crate. So Alda nursed it back to health. And in the end, it was hers and lived in a box near the dry well on her grandmother's island, spending the summer frolicking within the treetops.

The next autumn, the squirrel was gone. At first Alda had thought it found some warmer place to ride out the coldest months, but she had been mistaken.

One frosty morning, she discovered the dried remains of her animal friend near a rock pile at the far end of the island. Its sparse fur was matted with brown blood, its neck contorted at an unnatural angle. Parts were missing. It had been killed.

And as Alda stared at the squirrel's remains, she only wanted to kill the thing that had taken its life. But, helplessly, she knew she could not. Even if she could find the predator, she could not bring herself to harm it.

All these years later, Alda rarely thought of the squirrel because the image of its corpse overpowered any pleasant memories she had of the friendly creature. She only remembered it in death.

Now, looking at the dryads' remains, she felt the same stirrings of anger and vengeance combined with the knowledge that this, this would be her predominant memory of the magical beings. This is how she would forever see the dryads in her mind's eye.

Alda took a deep breath and summoned the courage to touch a branch. She remembered what the dryads had told her so long ago: their dead sister, the tree that had once held Ariel, still contained powers. So she bit her lip and, with pangs of regret, snapped a branch.

It turned to dust in her hand, blowing away in a sudden breeze.

So she instead examined the tree's trunk. It was cold, of course, and dry. Her fingertips ran over its surface, loosening pieces of bark that fell to the ground as powder.

On the smooth, white interior of the tree, crisscrossing over its surface, were marks burnt by some unknown flame. Strange lines seared in a complex pattern that reached up and down the tree. As Alda peeled more bark from its limbs, she saw an ever more intricate pattern of branching, irregular lines.

She had seen a pattern like this before. On Dreng. The red scar on his shoulder, the scar she had been too self-conscious to acknowledge out loud. To question. But she should have asked about its cause.

Because whatever had left its mark on Dreng had done the same to the dryads.

And she could guess what had caused this damage.

When Dreng was fighting the poison from Puck's blade, he fell in and out of consciousness, in and out of bewilderment. At times, he had spoken to his mother, mistaking Alda for the woman who had birthed him. Often, he swore and cursed at unseen sailors, thinking himself at sea.

But once or twice, he had whispered a chant and clutched his shoulder in agony.

Alda suspected the chant was more. Something wicked. Words of death and destruction. A spell.

And though Alda still knew relatively little of witchcraft, of the scope or scale of its powers or the numbers of those who practiced it, she guessed which three of its followers were likely culprits.

The weird sisters. They could have done this, destroyed the dryads and wrought havoc on the island. They could have done it, but did they?

And if they did, were they finished with their deed?

Or was worse yet to come?

Alda felt despondence overpower her, so she stood suddenly and wiped dripping water from her forehead. She was dizzy, tired. Somewhat disoriented. But she needed to persevere. To find a way home.

To find Dreng.

And she knew this place. So she pushed herself through the leafless forest. Over the stony fields. Up the grassless moors. And finally, after too many hours, the palazzo. Prospero's palazzo. Dilapidated. Abandoned. Still and quiet and void of colors. Like everything else in this cursed place.

Alda's feet dragged over the smooth stones of the palazzo's floor. The corridor smelled of wet decay. Holes in the roof let sun shine through, onto pockets of gray moss and brown leaves. She started down a corridor, changed direction, and turned again until she found herself in the library.

She remembered it from before, when she had learned that Miranda was Sycorax in disguise. When Alda hid from her, quaking with fear. And when Alda let loose her powers, shattering its massive windows and saving herself. When she searched Prospero's body and retrieved the miniature book, now missing in her flooded cottage.

But so much in the library had changed. The great Corinthian columns were crumbling, their stones pitted with time. The timbers above were warped and bent. The bookshelves were empty, their wooden planks battered and fallen into heaps. Not a book or manuscript or shred of parchment remained.

And in the center of the room was a great spiral. A witch-trap.

What had happened here, in her absence?

A snap. A jolt. And Alda felt her feet leave the floor and her back hit a toppled bookshelf.

She stood, stunned. Her ears ringing and shoulders aching. But she had to move, quickly, to avoid whatever invisible force had attacked her.

So she ran and ducked, sliding behind another bookshelf. It offered little protection as she peered through its shelves, searching for her adversary.

Another movement, like a wind, rattled a toppled bookcase across the room. And another. Like something was searching for prey, stalking to find her.

She ducked lower, her pulse racing. After several heartbeats of silence, she held her breath and again peered out, scanning the apparently empty library.

Except it was not empty. Movement caught her eye, in the far, shadowy corner. She squinted into the darkness and finally saw a faint flash of something. Hair? No. Skin? No.

Feathers.

And Alda felt a smile spread across her lips. She stood tentatively as she called out, "Ariel? Ariel, I mean you no harm!"

Silence.

She walked forward, slowly, avoiding the remains of the bookshelves and the spiral etched in stone.

"Ariel, I'm Alda. Show yourself. It is safe."

"This safety is a lie, but —"

A thud.

She saw him now, collapsed on the floor with his head propped against a wall, his great wings spread loosely at his sides. The harpy looked like a fallen angel from her grandmother's illustrated *Paradise Lost*, a celestial figure struck down by some mighty force.

"Where are the books? What killed the dryads? What happened here?" Her questions were soft and hurried as she rushed to his side.

But Ariel did not speak. Instead, he shifted until he was more upright. As she knelt at his side, she saw blood smeared across his cheek.

"What happened to you?"

"I thought you one of them." He sighed and added, "I'm nearly spent."

"Who did this?"

"They're gone. For now." His metric words were short, chopped, and he paused for breath at the end of each phrase.

"Who?" Alda lowered her voice as she guessed, "The witches?"

The harpy nodded, his breath rattling as he inhaled.

"What do they want?"

"A book. A book of spells." His eyes widened as he whispered, "The book of Prospero."

The miniature book, the tiny volume that contained the words to make the cauldron's bubble. Alda had last seen it in her cottage. Before she was whisked away by the rising waters of the Grand River.

Antediluvian. The word slipped into her head, inspired by the angel-like figure before her. *Before the flood.*

"Why do they want the book?"

Ariel coughed. "For knowledge. Power. All."

He coughed again, and more blood dripped from his mouth.

"Your injuries — Shall I help." Alda had intended it to be a question, but it came out with the force of a statement.

Another cough, deeper. "The island, its magic —" He gasped like a diver too long below water.

Alda reached for his hand. His claw-like fingers were cold, unmoving. "What can I do?"

Silence. Then, in a soft voice, "You tried to save me once before, and 'twas too early. Now, it's too late."

"No, no. What can I do, Ariel? Let me help you." A tear on her cheek. She cried too easily now for someone who was once so strong. She barely knew this creature, and their brief meetings had been born of mystery and violence.

"This is my island, child. Not Sycorax, nor Prospero, nor anyone could command it. Only I. And along with it, I must die."

"No, no, I can save it. Dreng, my friend — my friend and I will save it. And you. Please wait, Ariel. Wait before you, you sleep."

But it was too late. A shadow covered the sun, and the room turned to twilight shadows.

And instead of sadness, instead of grief, Alda only felt guilt. The harpy's energy was spent to attack her. If she had not come here... If she had announced herself... If she had never found the cauldron's bubble in the first place...

No. That would mean never meeting Dreng. She needed him in her life. She needed to find him.

And as she stood and turned from Ariel's motionless form, her thoughts leaped quickly from the harpy's death to what the future might hold.

How would she escape this place? Stop the witches? Return home?

More importantly, how would she find Dreng in the vast labyrinth of time and place without a cauldron's bubble?

Chapter Nine: Restless Ecstasy

The wet smell of the cave stung Dreng's nostrils as he followed closely behind Caliban when they passed from Netherfeld into the too-solid world.

"Do you need my hand, friend?" The words were heavy with sarcasm.

"Why did we not enter Netherfeld here before? Why did we take the raft to the Duke's Tree?"

"I did not know then what I know now."

"What is that?"

"My way."

Dreng only sighed. He continued walking in the dark, trusting the sound of his companion's footsteps more than his own instincts.

Caliban, Dreng knew, must understand these caves that connected Netherfeld to the world from which he came, the lightless tunnels that transected Prospero's island and bridged the land above with the realm of nothing.

Dreng, as well, had passed through one such cave after the flood, when he came into Netherfeld. So surely they must lead out as well.

Or was it another of Caliban's tricks?

Yet soon enough, Dreng saw a glimmer of light. A beam. Then an opening. The entrance to a cave. Not the grand cavern that had collapsed, but a lesser cave.

Smaller, narrower, lit with glowing jewels that sparkled like stars beneath their feet. They climbed up a steep slope, passing dripping water and eerie formations of slippery stone, until the weary travelers withdrew from a shallow hole near the island's clifftops.

The sun was a golden shimmer in the distance, like a piece of gold glittering above the sea. Dreng barely noticed. Caliban looked only to the ground as the pair persuaded their tired forms to silently take one step, and then another, until after too long they were nearly at the frozen spring that had so recently engulfed Sycorax's body.

But was it indeed recent? The trees in the forest's edge drooped, their limbs barren and bark stripped. The grasses of the open moors were brown and brittle. No foliage. No life. No birds or bees or sounds. The island was desolate. Dead. Silent.

Dreng remembered the too-familiar songs that he heard nightly when he lived in the palace. They were so common that they became like a breath, nearly unheard.

But now, the sounds' absence was deafening.

As silent as the grave.

A fitting turn of phrase for what appeared before them: Sycorax — or rather Miranda's body — entombed in a shallow pool of clear ice. Her form still, in a magical sleep. Or death. Like a living statue that had lost its animation. Not aged or broken or decayed. The same as when Dreng had last beheld her. Unmoving and unmoved.

As Dreng knelt next to the frozen spring, he ran his fingers over the surface. He could break the ice or melt it with a flame, but then what? Her body had been injured, perhaps destroyed, in the collapse of the cavern. Could they resuscitate her? Or had so many weeks, or months, or years, made this an eternal tomb?

"We need a spell." Caliban's quiet, uncertain words broke Dreng's reverie. Since they had returned to the island, Caliban had barely uttered a sentence. Now his tone was distant, soft. Lacking the charisma and sarcasm that usually weighed his words.

"What spell?"

Caliban sighed, the wrinkles near his eyes somehow becoming deeper. "I do not know. *She* would know. But she is not here..."

Dreng was unsure if he spoke of Sycorax or Miranda, but it mattered naught. He looked up the hill to the palace above, its form vastly more ruinous than when they had left on the raft.

How much time had passed when they were away, in Fairy Land and Netherfeld?

"Should we go to the palace's library?"

"Perhaps." Caliban wiped his eyes and, for what was likely the first time, admitted, "I don't know what to do. Without a spell, the pearl —"

"Perhaps this will help." Dreng set his jaw as he retrieved the miniature book from the folds at his waist and passed it to Caliban.

"Where, where did you get this?"

"Alda."

Caliban smiled, "She is a witch and a thief. No wonder you love her."

"I — I don't. I mean, I —"

Caliban silenced his protest with a wave of his hand. "It matters not." He thumbed through the tiny pages, searching.

Finally, he landed on his mark. Pointing, he handed the book back to Dreng. "Read this, *paramour*."

Dreng scowled but did as he was told and read a spell entitled "trouble fire:" "Come deadly flames to charm the air and cast about the mortals' games, to take from each his deathly share and cloud the sun, until the hurley-burley's done."

As Dreng spoke, Caliban held his hand, the pearl clasped between their palms. When Dreng finished, he waited, his breath shallow. Nothing.

Caliban shifted away and rubbed his fingers nervously. Moments passed. Caliban stood and peered at the ice. Then he paced, the blue cloak flapping rhythmically against his legs.

And Dreng remembered the words of his father's

ghost: "The changeling, beyond the tree, can save her."
He had assumed the changeling was Alda, somehow, so
perhaps they needed her to revive Sycorax.

Or he was the changeling. Or Caliban.

Or the ghost was wrong. Or deceitful.

After several excruciating minutes, Caliban turned to
Dreng with a cruel sneer, "You must have tripped on your
tongue. Read again, and speak apace."

But before Dreng could repeat the spell, they both
leapt back in surprise. Above the frozen spring was an
orb, its surface burning in green-red flames. A wisp, like
the Irish sailors had described in their tales of fairies and
little people. It quickly spread and fell onto the ice, its
flames growing taller and transforming into deep, blood-
red. It suddenly burst into a white light, and then vanished.

Dreng blinked as his eyes adjusted to the scene
before him: the spring was a low, liquid pool, barely
ankle-deep. Steam rose from its surface. Within the
shroud of mist, Miranda's form convulsed as white foam
trickled from her lips.

Before Dreng could react, Caliban was at her side,
cradling her head as her limbs thrashed uncontrollably.
He looked to Dreng helplessly, "Help me hold her!"

Dreng took her shoulders and eased them up until
her torso was well above the water. As Caliban stroked
her hair, Dreng could see that her eyeballs were streaked

in red, unseeing and flicking unnaturally.

Despite her uncontrollable ferocity, Caliban calmly soothed, "This is home, Mother, you are safe, open your eyes —"

Dreng was helpless, as was Caliban, who continued to speak softly, his words either prayers or curses.

And Dreng expected the worst. When he had placed his wife's body in the spring, when its waters enveloped her form, she was injured. Gravely. And even though Caliban expected some miraculous cure, some resurrection, Dreng had his doubts. Surely mere waters could not sustain a person so long. Surely she could not be healed.

But suddenly, the body of the blonde girl took a deep breath and relaxed as heat radiated from her form. In the still quiet of the evening, Dreng could hear her voice fill with happiness as she whispered, "Cali?"

The beautiful youth first recoiled and then bent forward, touching her neck tenderly as tears welled in his eyes, and Dreng turned his face to hide the conflicting emotions in his eyes.

This was not Sycorax. This was someone much kinder, younger. Someone whom Caliban knew.

A trick, indeed.

"Miranda..." Caliban's voice shook with emotion. "I can't — I can't — Now, I —"

Dreng knew he should be happy for his friend. And

besides, perhaps Miranda could help them stop the witches. She could have yet unknown magic, after all.

But Caliban's voice shook with emotion. Not hope. Not love. Desperation. "Not now, my once-love. It is not your time." Caliban's voice grew louder as he spoke a string of words. A spell. The same he had muttered when he resurrected Miranda in his cave.

And as Dreng watched the pair, the girl sat bolt upright as red light swirled around her form. It quickly faded, and she looked to the sky and blinked, then stepped from the shallow pool and stretched her arms above her head as one awaking from a long slumber.

As Caliban hung his head and quietly wiped tears from his eyes, Dreng was again struck by how his companion's face had changed. More somber, yes, but also aged. Worn. No, forlorn.

The yellow-haired girl looked first to him and then to Dreng. "We have work, my boys." Her tone was icy, condescending. "The witches are coming. They're close. And we must strike first." Her eyes flashed. Blue eyes. Sycorax's eyes.

And in that moment, Dreng regretted waking the woman he once loved. But, still, he needed her. To find Alda. But what would be the price of her help?

*   *   *

Alda, alone in the vacant library of the crumbling palazzo, felt her body become limp, numb. She was tired. No, exhausted. No, beyond even that. Bone-dead tired, her grandmother would have said.

Bone. Dead. Tired.

Ariel was dead. She had come here, so many months ago, to find him. To free him or capture him or somehow bring him to the witches on the moor. She had a goal then. A purpose. And now, she was helpless. Without a path forward.

She could not bring herself to look at the harpy's body across the room, breathless and motionless. Still, she felt safer with him nearby. As if the form of the great harpy might drive away any threat. A rouse. A trick.

Her mind wandered again to the witches. To the fear she felt before them in Netherfeld. To her mother's spirit-form, trapped in the void. To Miranda. To Dreng.

Her thoughts became swift and disconnected, the flashes of her memories and wishes as she lingered between awareness and sleep.

Images from her stereopticon cards. The Sphinx. Parthenon. Colosseum. Then they became more real, recollections of her life in Grand Ledge. The Folly Hotel. The Opera House. The Ledge Path. Alda's hand passing over the tourists' graffiti, etched into the sandstone cliffs. Names.

Dates. Initials. Hearts. A cowboy with a pipe. A chief with a feathered headdress. A mermaid holding an anchor.

Then the carving on her grandmother's gravestone: Able Reeding. Alda's fingers running over that, too. And the name changed before her mind's eye, its letters reworking themselves: Hecate. And Alda was alone in the cemetery. An open grave before her with a new stone above its void. Blank. No name. No date. Alda peered inside and saw a mirror. No reflection on its surface.

She was suddenly back in her cottage. Orange and red and yellow leaves outside. The colors of autumn. And flames. And heat. Sudden heat. Not from the fireplace, but from Alda's hands. Burning. Engulfing her. Surrounded by fire.

And Alda choked amid the black smoke as it burned her eyes and scorched her skin. She was burning alive. Combusting. Searing. And she could not move. Frozen.

But then she gasped. Clean air. Again. And again. And. Again. Until her breath became even. Calm. Until she awoke in the reality of the palazzo's empty library.

Long beams of light pierced the broken windows, streaming down from holes above.

Alda was safe. For now. And alone. Again. She shivered in the darkness, goosebumps forming on her sweat-drenched skin.

And then she cried. Not the silent tears she felt on

her cheeks so many times before. Not the tears of sorrow she wept over Dreng. But the wailing howls of a caged animal. A bereft mother. A lost soul.

She cried until the tears turned hot on her skin. Until her hands shook and her throat ached.

Until she no longer felt like a girl trapped in the hands of fate but like a woman who could control her own destiny.

And then she stopped, wiped her face, and stood. She had to move. To do something. To find Dreng. To stop the witches. To get home, safely, to her cottage.

She shut her eyes, focusing only on her goals and wishes, and she felt a rush of wind, as she had so long ago when the windows shattered at her command. Her hands felt warm, powerful.

And when Alda again opened her eyes, her fingertips glowed with a fierce, white light.

Chapter Ten: Strange Bedfellows

Dreng strained to follow Sycorax in the waning light as she raced up the hill to the palace. He could not match her speed.

He remembered so many months before, after she had returned from Netherfeld with her fiery spirits. How he had loved her then. No, worshipped her. And the memory brought shame. Dreng blushed, despite himself.

He regretted being so easily susceptible to her apparent spell. To falling so quickly. And for a flash, he wished that he had never known her. That he had immediately lashed together the broken planks of *The Tempest* and set out that same day onto the sea.

He might have died, yes, but he might have lived. Reached a port. Found a place in a new crew. Returned to sea again. The same. Unchanged.

But then he would never have known the wonders he had seen since. Fairy Land. Netherfeld. Or Alda.

A life without Alda was not worth living. So, in the end, his past lapse was worth his current regret.

Now, as Dreng watched Sycorax approach the palace, he realized her pace was something more than mortal. Caliban soon fell behind and finally settled into step alongside Dreng, adjusting his sapphire cloak as they walked.

"You are angry?" It might have been a simple observation, but Caliban's voice rose questioningly, seeking an answer.

Dreng clenched his jaw as he thought of wide-eyed Miranda awaking from the frozen waters. "I do not understand you."

"I am beyond comprehension."

"No, what you did at the spring."

Caliban sighed. "We need my mother *now*, Dreng. She knows —"

"And what of Miranda?"

Caliban lowered his voice. "She could not help."

"But she came back, to you, and you, you did what with her?"

Caliban avoided his accusatory stare and looked up to the figure outpacing them.

"And for *her*?" Dreng shook his head in frustration. "You traded the woman you loved for your mother."

"You loved her once."

"That spell is gone." Dreng had felt it lift on the raft. And now, it had no hold on him.

Caliban glanced at him. "She is more powerful than any of us."

Dreng scowled.

"And she is your wife."

"She is not."

"Denial does not make it less true."

Dreng shook his head and studied the ground as he walked. "And what of Miranda?"

"I returned her to Netherfeld."

"You mean you exiled her soul and stole her body."

Caliban stopped and caught Dreng's shoulder. "She is safe there. And I will rescue her, soon, as Orpheus led Eurydice from the jaws of Hades."

Dreng felt confusion flash across his face, so Caliban sighed and explained, "I will lead Miranda from Netherfeld into our world, as I led you through the caves. When it is safe here. But until then… Without Sycorax, our world may cease to exist."

Dreng shook his head, "You trust Sycorax, but —"

"I do not trust her. Nor should you. But use logic. My mother has awoken from the place of nothing after how long? Years? She has seen the witches there, and has heard whispers of their plan. She *knows* them, knows them from before I came to be. And, like us, she wants them destroyed. More than we. So we *need* her if we want to save this world. Regardless of trust."

Dreng's shoulders slumped as he relented. He felt weak, beaten down, ready to surrender. "I understand, but I cannot obey her."

"Then trust me."

Despite himself, Dreng laughed. "You ask the

impossible."

Caliban likewise grinned. "Then simply do not die."

"As always."

They shared a smile. But Dreng's grin quickly faded to concern as they reached the doorway of the crumbled palace.

As they passed over the threshold, Dreng caught a flash of the palace from the time it had been his residence: warm and candlelit, the scent of Mediterranean herbs overpowering the salt of seawater, the soft tread of Miranda's footstep echoing down the corridor.

But that was a mirage, both then and now. He had never known Miranda. It had always been Sycorax, disguised in a stolen form. And now, the truth was before him: crumbling stones and the smell of cold, wet decay. Nothing warm. Nothing loving. Nothing safe. All ruins.

Yet soft footsteps echoed down the corridor.

The trio stopped, their silence shared as they listened.

The steps were hurried but light. Caliban started forward, but Dreng held out his arm.

"I know more stealth than you. Give me your sword, and I will find whatever danger waits ahead."

Caliban shook his head and whispered, "Sword? No. This will do." He retrieved a dagger from a concealed lashing around his calf and thrust its hilt into Dreng's palm. "Something of this size is more fitting for you."

Dreng scowled as he positioned the dagger in his right hand, his boots nearly silent against the cold stones as he turned a corner and lost sight of Caliban and Sycorax.

He traced the sound to the library. Hurried footsteps, seemingly back and forth. Pacing. Sighs. Heavy breaths. As he grew closer, he heard muttering. Angry. Guttural. Like a caged animal. Yet familiar.

He stood against the wall outside the library's doorway and listened. When the footsteps were at the farthest end of the room, he ducked inside, expecting to conceal himself behind a bookshelf.

But the shelves were likewise in ruins. The seemingly endless rows of volumes were gone.

Dreng moved quickly to the far wall and hid within shadows. Beside him, half-reclined in a corner, was the lifeless form of the harpy Ariel.

Ariel. Here. Dead.

Dreng knew not to gasp. He knew not to show surprise. Or hesitation. Or fear.

But whatever had killed the harpy was more powerful than any being Dreng before had encountered.

Holding his breath, Dreng bit his tongue as he watched the murderous figure across the room, its back turned toward him. It glowed in an unnatural, brilliant, white radiance. Sparks trickled from its fingers. Ethereal. A spirit? A ghost?

It turned, and its black hair swirled. Inky black. Like midnight. And Dreng knew, "Alda!"

He leapt from the corner and ran to her. She hesitated at first and stepped back, the white glow disappearing as she returned to her normal, familiar self.

They spoke at once, their words overlapping.

"How did you get here?"

"What happened?"

"Where were you?"

"Were you in Netherfeld?"

"Did you see the witches?"

"Are you hurt?"

"You killed Ariel?"

"No, I, I —"

"Why were you glowing?" Dreng realized that his left hand was upon her waist, the dagger still clenched in his other fist, and he stepped back self-consciously.

Alda likewise blushed and looked away before her voice took on a skeptical tone. "Glowing?" She laughed. "I was warm, yes, flushed perhaps. But glowing?" Her cheeks burned crimson as she shyly met his eyes.

"It was —" He searched for a word and, unable to think of one better, whispered, "Magical."

Alda's brow furrowed, and the corners of her mouth bent down slightly. "I, I don't know. I wasn't aware I — I was only thinking about you and how to find you and how

I am trapped on this blasted island, and then my fingers, well, they — well, here *you* are." She smiled, and his heart eased somewhat. "Do you have half of the cauldron's bubble?"

He nodded. "And you?"

Her smile broadened. "In my sock. We can combine the parts somehow, I suspect, and use it again to escape and —"

Alda stopped suddenly as Dreng summoned the courage to take her hand and, squeezing her fingers, said, "I am glad to be here, with you, but, but —" He glanced over his shoulder and quickly dropped her hand as he concealed Caliban's dagger within his boot. "We are not alone."

"What do you mean? Who else is —" Alda could not finish.

Sycorax burst into the room, her golden hair whipping as she rushed Alda and felled her with a powerful blow.

Dreng was torn between helping the victim and stopping the aggressor but quickly held Sycorax back as she readied for a second swing.

Alda lifted herself from the ground and rubbed her bleeding cheek. Caliban tried to wipe her blood with a corner of his sleeve, but she pushed him away and looked to Dreng as a condemned man might glare at his accuser.

He held firm to Sycorax's arms, knowing full well

that she could level him with a magical word. Still, he did not let go.

Finally, Sycorax ceased her struggle. "Here you are, *dear* friend! Always interfering. Always standing in my way. Always under foot." She stomped, and the palace quaked as more stones crumbled from its walls.

Sycorax twisted free from Dreng's grasp and again rushed at Alda, but Caliban stood between the two women. Alda looked to both sides, searching for an escape, as Sycorax pointed threateningly at her face.

Sparks erupted from the summoner's fingertip. "You have done nothing but deceive and betray me, girl, and it is time now to —"

Dreng started toward them, but Caliban pushed his mother's hand aside and hissed, "Not now. We need this one's help." He glanced nervously at the corner where Ariel's body was slumped and added, "The books are gone. We are alone. She is all that we have here, now. Do not kill our only ally."

Sycorax spat and turned her back to the others, her arms crossed and her foot tapping angrily. Finally, she faced them and smiled threateningly as one might at a naughty child, an expression Dreng had seen so many times before when they were together on the island.

He looked away as his wife explained, "The witches are growing stronger by the minute. And these three are not simply magical women. They are of the ancient times, of fate and destiny and elemental knowledge. And in those ancient times, some force — some god or act of nature — bound our world together with magic. So all that is invisible — love and honor and sacrifice, hope, knowledge, joy — are made up of this primordial magic. And all physical things contain some traces of it as well. So when it vanishes, when the witches have destroyed all magic, we are left with nothing."

Caliban nodded, "Like my decaying tower in Netherfeld. All the worlds will be gone, flung into chaos."

Dreng clenched his jaw.

Sycorax smiled at her son, sincerely, "Yes, the state of confusion that existed before order. These weird women are of that. Or perhaps they made it. And now they want it to return."

Dreng glanced at Alda, saw her backing away from the others into the shadow of a toppled bookshelf. She wanted to be unseen, so he asked skeptically, drawing attention to himself, "What happens if they succeed, if magic disappears?"

"Chaos is a state of nothing, you puppet." Caliban smirked. "You would be a part of it as well."

Dreng turned his back to Caliban and faced Sycorax instead. "How do you know that is the witches' goal?"

The woman he once loved glanced at him and

quickly averted her gaze, shaking her head as she seemed to study her feet. After several deep breaths, she straightened and faced Dreng again, her chin held unnaturally high. "Do you know who I am?"

"Sycorax." The name still sounded forced, and she lowered her head slightly at the sound.

"No, that is what I am called now. But that is not who I *am*." She avoided his eyes and paced, her feet scattering dust from the toppled shelves. "I was young once, in love."

She glanced at him, and Dreng bit his tongue. The word stung, but he remained silent, so she continued, "I was called Ophelia then, and the man I loved — Caliban's father — was mad. To save him, I aligned myself with the weird sisters. And then, even then, they wanted chaos. They destroyed me. And him. They meddle in the lives of mortals, until there is nothing but disorder. That, somehow, brings them peace. Or…" She paused. "But they do not think as we do. They are elemental. And dangerous. And when I was trapped in the frozen pool, they grasped their chance and started to seize power."

She stopped pacing and whispered, with too bitter tears in her eyes, "The witches bring only death and despair. Without them, I would still have my Hamlet."

Dreng stumbled back at the name, "Who?" But she did not meet his gaze. "You were — what you said —" Caliban had spoken truth about his parentage. This woman — his mother — and the Danish prince. And Dreng felt a pang of regret for not believing the beautiful youth sooner as he realized, "On the ship, Hamlet spoke of a lost love."

She smiled weakly and stepped closer to him as her demeanor changed to something calm and soothing. "When I first saw you, Dreng, I recognized *his* ring. He would never lose it, never barter with it, never let it be taken by violence. Since you had it, I knew that he gave it to you freely. That you were a good man. That I could trust you. So help me now. Believe me. About the witches. Despite what has passed between us."

She reached for his hand, and he did not immediately pull it away. Her fingers were icy, foreign on his. A memory, once joyful and now forlorn.

He retrieved his hand and held his fists behind his back. "We need Alda."

Sycorax sneered, "You may, but *I* do not." She glanced at Alda, who hid in the shadows some distance behind Caliban, rubbing her cheek and glaring at the others.

"The Indian boy is right."

Dreng glared at Caliban, who continued, "And she is powerful enough to kill a harpy."

Alda's voice cracked, "I did not! Ariel, he —"

Sycorax held her palm upright to stop Alda as she spoke to Dreng. "Why do you need her?"

"She glows."

Chapter Eleven: Insubstantial Pageant

Alda hoped that Dreng was mistaken. That she was not a necessary tool to fight the witches. After all, she felt no different when she had apparently glowed, apart from a brief sensation of heat. She had seen no light emanate from her body, only white illuminating her fingertips. She seemed as she had always been — not entirely normal, but not overtly magical.

And she still hoped that she could escape with Dreng and forsake Sycorax and Caliban to battle the witches themselves.

So when Dreng revealed her apparent ability to the others, his betrayal stung.

"She glows?" Sycorax eyed Alda like a wildcat about to pounce.

Alda stood behind Caliban as she admitted, "I might have some magic in me, but I cannot use it. Not well. Not well enough, at least."

Caliban turned to her, and she was startled by the sincerity in his eyes. "Some is better than naught." He rifled through his clothing and retrieved a small, white bead.

Sycorax grinned, "You found it."

"How do you think you were awoken, Mother?"

"Let me have it!"

"I know what *you* would do with it, but I want to see

how it reacts with the witch."

He held it before her in his palm, but Alda refused the offer and instead asked, "What is it?"

"The pearl of wisdom. It intensifies magic."

"Where did you get it?"

Dreng looked away, his face revealing some inner turmoil.

Caliban explained, "From Prospero's staff."

Alda spat, "When you killed him."

"I? Never! And I have a witness." Caliban's face was a mockery of innocence as he turned to Dreng, who meekly nodded. "See? Now, take it. Then we'll all know what powers you hold."

Alda still hesitated. This was too much. Dreng's sudden appearance had been welcomed. Wanted. And she had so much to tell him. So much to say. But now, now, with the others... She could not speak her mind. And she was not in control. Once again, she could only act on the whims of those around her.

Alda was aware of Sycorax's defiant stare, her arms crossed angrily below Miranda's tumble of yellow hair. Dreng watched her anxiously, his fingers fidgeting at his sides. Caliban again thrust his open palm toward her, so Alda held her breath as she touched the pearl with a shaking finger.

A rumble, low and deep. And then higher, closer, its

pitch rising and its intensity increasing. An earthquake. No, more. As the ground shook, the air grew hot and thick. Lightning. Simultaneous thunder. And in a fraction of an instant, a shot of cold reverberated from Alda's hand as white light enveloped the ruined library. The ground heaved, and then all was dust and blackness.

Alda felt pain on her back first, weight from the roof's timbers that pressed her down. Her head was protected, her hands wrapped instinctually above it. One ankle trapped, but the other free. She kicked the wall-stone that held her in place and reached up through the debris of the collapsed palazzo until her fingers pierced sunlight above. And she pulled. And pushed. And heaved herself free from the rubble.

As she brushed the dust and blinked in the dimming light, she saw that Dreng was already standing above the ruins, his feet on a great column as he reached into the depths to pull Sycorax free, her fingers clasping his wrist. As he helped the summoner to safety, he looked up and saw Alda. His expression changed.

"You're injured."

She felt a drip between her eyes and smeared blood across her forehead. "A scratch." Yet she felt dizzy and closed her eyes as she repeated, "A scratch. It's not so deep."

But she slumped onto the rubble for a moment, the world spinning before her, and surveyed the ruins. She felt like a lone survivor after some devastating war, or like the first woman thrust out from paradise and into desolation.

However, she was not alone. Dreng was quickly at her side, Sycorax sitting some distance behind him, similarly shocked and stone-faced.

"Where is Caliban?"

"He was here, before me, when I touched the pearl."

Both Alda and Dreng leapt to the place and reached into the rubble.

Alda's fingers found him first, his blood-wet clothes cold against her fingers. As she dug, with prayers unspoken on her lips, she saw the rubble likewise stained red.

Dreng removed debris relentlessly, silently, until Alda could see Caliban's swollen and bloodied face emerge from the ruins. They extracted him together and carefully carried him across the ruins to the open space of the courtyard. Dreng gently placed him on a long-stone that had once encircled the fountain's pool — the fountain that Alda had destroyed during the fiery storm so many months ago — and Alda wrapped Caliban in his torn and dusty cloak.

And then they waited.

Alda stood beside the injured youth, her hand on his bleeding forehead. She looked at Dreng and remembered the care she gave him in her cottage. The worry and panic. The same feelings fell upon her now, but less intense. Less powerful.

Still, she feared. For some moments, Caliban's
breaths were irregular. The three watched in silence as
they became more shallow, barely audible. His chest
barely moving.

Then, they ceased.

Silence.

Sycorax stood in shock, her hands on her stomach
and tears streaming down her cheeks. "He cannot leave
me, he cannot leave me..." she repeated again and again.

Dreng turned away and covered his face.

Alda, however, remained at Caliban's side, his hand
clasped in hers. She was surprisingly calm, not frightened
or panicked. Yet there was hope. There was always hope.
So instead of weeping or cursing, she whispered into his
ear, "She is alive, still. Miranda. I saw her, and she needs
you." Alda waited and thought she felt something like a
flutter in his palm. "Caliban, Miranda needs you. She
needs you. We need you. Come back. For us."

A tear fell down Alda's cheek, trickled down her chin
and onto her neck. She released Caliban's hand to wipe it
away, but more tears quickly followed. She hid her face
in the folds of her skirt until a cough broke her sorrow.
Then a deep, rattling breath.

Finally, "If I return from the dead, it will be for my
own sake. Not for you lot of foot-lickers."

Alda did not expect such a flood of relief, not for someone who was at best a stranger and at worst an enemy. But she wiped his face with her sleeve until he pushed her away and sat wobbling atop the long-stone.

Dreng turned pale at the sudden resurrection, and Sycorax's shoulders relaxed beneath her faded dress.

Caliban stared at them as if they were lunatics until he finally spat, "Why is the witch more moved by my rising than are my kin?"

Alda wiped the remainder of her tears and laughed, "I am not a witch."

Sycorax knelt at her side and, glancing at Caliban, took Alda's hand. "But you *are*. And we need your help."

Alda looked at the others, all staring expectantly at her. Dreng with his quiet hope. Sycorax with her intensity. Caliban, bloodied and destitute. She could not disappoint them or abandon them. She could not take Dreng and flee with the cauldron's bubble. She had to stay and fight.

So, as resolutely as she could, Alda nodded. "What should we do?"

Caliban inspected the wounds on his chest and arms and then sadly examined his bent sword as Sycorax spoke: "The witches have drained this island. And nearly Netherfeld. And, most likely, the worlds beyond as well."

Alda felt her eyes widen. How many worlds were there? But she was silent as the summoner continued,

"We must find them. And soon. But it will take ages to discover them in the web of realms."

Dreng cleared his throat. "We need a trap."

"A trap?" Caliban scoffed, "No cage will hold them, you lily-liver." He pressed his foot on his blade, trying unsuccessfully to bend it back into shape.

Dreng retorted, "You should not turn the tip like that, you... egg."

"You speak of country matters," Caliban spat.

Dreng scowled, turned from him, and continued, "But surely our combined magic can hold the witches at bay. And with Alda's help —" He looked at her with a mixture of hope and something else. "We only have to lure them here."

Caliban angrily sheathed his sword, its blade still bent. "And how should we call them? Ask politely? Say *please*? Whisper our wishes into the wind and hope they hear?"

Dreng frowned. "They want *me*, remember. In Netherfeld, you saw them —"

Alda gasped. "You confronted the witches?"

But Dreng continued, "They wanted something from me. Let me be your bait. I will call them, somehow."

Caliban's tone lost its notes of sarcasm. "Somehow is the dilemma."

Alda thought back to the last time she encountered Sycorax on the island, of the spirits the summoner used to storm the palazzo. For a moment, Alda thought that might work again, and then she blushed. Now that she knew the truth, now that she understood that those spirits were enslaved from Netherfeld, she could not suggest such a feat. And she regretted having summoned them herself. She bit her lip, trying to think of some alternative.

"We need a spell." Sycorax's face was stern, distant. "But the library, it —" She looked at the rubble behind them. "I do not know such magic. Not by heart."

She looked at Alda questioningly. "I, I don't —" Alda studied her feet, avoiding the enquiring gazes of the others.

Dreng placed his hand reassuringly on Alda's shoulder. "I have your book."

He reached within the folds at his waist and retrieved the miniature book, the volume Alda had taken from Prospero's body in the library. The book that Alda had thought was lost in the flood. It was safe. And her shock shifted quickly to relief.

Sycorax smiled, and Caliban looked up from his unhappy sword.

As Alda's mind raced, her three companions said at once, "I have a plan."

*   *   *

They laid out ideas, their words weaving over and through their thoughts until three separate plans slowly became one.

"But we need the pearl of wisdom for this to work." Dreng's heart sank as he realized it was likely in the rubble, lost amid the broken stones and cracked timber.

But Caliban laughed, the sound quickly becoming a cough as he bent over and clutched his stomach. He spat, wiped blood from his mouth, and shuddered as he straightened himself. In his open palm was the pearl of wisdom. "I may be rather grave, but I still have a grip."

Dreng smiled despite himself and looked to Alda, "When they arrive, you must take the pearl and —"

"No." Alda's tone was resolute. "I touched it once, and nearly killed us all. I will not do so again." Her voice became softer, pleading, "I will face the witches to protect you." She looked to Caliban and Sycorax. "But I know that whatever magic I perform will be instinctual. I cannot control it. That jewel, that pearl is dangerous in my hand. Dangerous to us all."

"Then I will use it." Sycorax was too eager, and Dreng wanted to object, but he held his tongue as she took the pearl from Caliban. "The witches once taught me a spell that I can use against them, if it comes to that. And Dreng, what of you? Do you know what to do?"

He nodded. Two spells in the book seemed the most likely to lead to their success, or their survival: "pricking thumb" to summon the witches, and "trouble fire" to stun them.

Then Alda and Sycorax and Caliban would finish them, each in their own way.

"Well, what are we waiting for? Let's call the blasted devils and save the world!" Caliban stood, with his bent sword in hand, and struck a pose that Dreng could only assume was meant to be heroic. But he swooned like a man sick at sea, doubled over, and fell to his knees.

Before Dreng or Sycorax could react, Alda was at his side with her arm around his shoulders. She eased him back onto the rock, wiped the wounds on his head with a corner of her skirt, and spoke softly, too softly for Dreng to hear.

But he could see the kindness in her eyes, the care that she gave even to someone who had wronged her in the past. She looked like one of the haloed figures whose paintings were prized by Spanish sailors: all peace and forgiveness and compassion. And he knew that his friend was safe with her.

Finally, Alda looked to Dreng. "He needs water."

"I will fetch some." Again, Sycorax was too eager. She started to pick her way over the ruins as Dreng turned to Alda, nodded, and followed the summoner away from the ruined palace.

Dreng still did not trust Sycorax. Especially when she would so soon command something as powerful as the pearl of wisdom.

Besides, Dreng had no purpose at the moment. He felt breathless as he watched Alda with Caliban, like someone swept overboard in rough seas. His emotions were in his throat, dangerously near to suffocating him. So he pushed them down. For now, at least.

"There is rainwater trapped upon the rocks at the cliff's edge."

Sycorax's words startled him, and his mind seemed to snap to attention as she led the way toward some great stones.

"Should we go to the spring instead?"

"No." Sycorax averted her gaze. "Those waters are… too powerful."

Dreng doubted her words but did not protest. He instead looked out to sea as she bent over the hollows and filled a dented pewter mug with clear water.

"Where did you get that?"

"From the ruins." She smiled at him, the way she always did when his foolishness amused her. "Your mind is elsewhere, Dreng."

"It is not. I, I only —"

"You love her."

The words were not a question. Sycorax stood at his side, her eyes studying his as she took a draught from the mug.

"I — I do not know what love is."

"I am, I am sorry." Sincere remorse permeated her words as she filled the mug.

Dreng shifted his gaze from the sea and looked instead at his boots, their leather scuffed and coated in dust from the crumbled palace.

He could feel Sycorax's eyes on him as she continued, "Dreng, I did not wish for this. Any of it."

"Nor did I." He did not attempt to conceal the loathing in his voice.

"I — I am sorry. For the spell —"

"Curse."

"Dishonesty —"

"Deception."

"I did love you, once."

Dreng scowled. "Lies."

Sycorax lowered her tone and leaned toward his ear. "Those months with you, here, as my husband —"

"Do not call me that."

"With you, that was the happiest time since — since I came to this island."

His anger lifted somewhat as he realized she was right. He had been happy as well. But he could not speak the words, he could not vocalize agreement, so he only nodded.

She continued, "Yet that time is past. And we are here. Now."

They stood in silence. Dreng felt his pulse quicken as he realized that he was trapped. "Release me."

"What?"

Dreng took her hand as one begging an executioner for mercy. "We had a rite, a ceremony. We are married, still, in some way. Even though the curse is passed. Even though I — I —"

"I know you did not love me. Not truly. It was all a deception. So those words you shared with me, the words that bound us one to another, were not honest. They had no truth. They were like lines in a play, spoken by someone performing a part."

She held both of his hands in hers, as she had so many months ago in the courtyard of Prospero's palace, when he wanted nothing more than to be her husband and to be bound to her for eternity.

"Forget them, Dreng. Forget the words, the rite. Forget our lives together. Forget me." She squeezed his palms, and he likewise pressed his fingers into hers. "I suspect you would be luckier now, if not for me." Sycorax glanced at the nearby palace, at the figures of Alda and Caliban, their forms huddled close. "You can find happiness yet."

Dreng released her hands and wiped his brow. "Happiness is not my lot." He felt regret cross his face for a moment but quickly set his jaw, hoping resolve would conceal his true feelings, his sense of foreboding.

"What do you intend to do?" Her tone echoed that of the ship's captain, commanding and earnest.

"I cannot let her come to harm." He licked his lips, suddenly dry. "I must protect her, Sycorax. If all else — Alda must be safe."

The summoner's voice lowered to a quiver. "No, Dreng. That is not your lot. We will all survive."

But Dreng could see the lie behind her eyes, the sadness and acceptance, and he understood.

Dreng clenched his jaw. "What should we do?"

Sycorax smiled.

Chapter Twelve: Mercy Itself

Caliban was silent as Alda tended to the blood seeping from the wound on his head. She could sense that he did not wish to speak. But she could not remain silent, so she began, "This will be over soon, one way or another. And we will all be safe, or dead."

"The dead are safe," he muttered.

"Then we cannot lose." She smiled at him, and his glare eased somewhat. So she continued, "Were you in Netherfeld, all this time?"

"Yes, and no."

Alda waited for him to elaborate, but he did not. Instead, he merely twisted the hem of the blue cloak nervously in his fingers.

"And were you alone there?"

"Yes, and no."

Again, several heartbeats of silence.

"I was in Netherfeld as well." Alda paused, waiting, and continued, "And I was not alone."

"I suppose you were not, witch. I expect you had spirits you could control, to do your bidding. Like my mother. Were they your slaves as well?" He slung the words like weapons, but Alda did not recoil as she sat at his side.

"I saw her, Caliban. I saw your Miranda."

He stopped fidgeting. But he still did not meet her gaze.

"She told me — She told me that she cared for you. Always. Despite how you — how you once appeared."

"No, she could not care for me. That was a lie, taught to her by her father, to be cruel to me."

Alda disregarded his objections and continued, "And she told me that on that day, the day I arrived on this island, she was going to you."

"To torture me further."

"To tell you that she loved you."

Caliban broke. His hands shook as he reached for his face, concealing the tears on his cheeks. Alda was stunned for a moment, surprised by his sudden and unexpected change. She had thought him incapable of powerful emotions, numb with sarcasm and wit.

So she wrapped her arms around his shoulders, bent close to his ear, and whispered, "She is waiting for you in Netherfeld. And she believes you will find her, now that you know she still loves you. And that she has always loved you. She will be there for you, waiting until you arrive."

There was more, but Alda could not bring herself to speak of Miranda's dealings with the witches. She was likely an innocent, lured in by them as Ophelia had once been duped. And that would be for naught soon enough, when the witches were gone.

Caliban finally looked up, and his eyes met hers, their orbs filled with heartbreak and regret. "Alda, I, I had her, here, for a moment, and I —" He hung his head. "I didn't know why she was on the beach that day. I never, never would have..." His voice faded, his final words lost in a deep breath.

"It's not too late, Caliban. You can go to her."

"Now? But you need me. For the witches."

"You are too injured."

"I am not!" He attempted to rise again, but his legs gave way beneath him.

"See? And what can you do that we cannot?"

"I can do many great and mysterious things."

Alda laughed as she wiped a tear from her friend's eye.

His tone grew more serious. "Alda, let me stand with you. There is too much at stake — We could all die."

Alda shook her head. "And if you try to fight now, *you will* die."

Caliban looked toward the sea, toward Sycorax and Dreng bent over a great rock above the cliffs. "I can fetch her, Alda. Bring Miranda here so she can help us." His voice rose with excitement. "I can reach her through the caves and bring her back, leading her like Orpheus out of the underworld."

Alda frowned. "I know that myth. It does not end well."

"But this is different. If I go to her now, quickly, I can return to fight. We can return together." He shifted his gaze again and looked imploringly at Alda. "Will you wait until I return?"

Alda lied, "Of course."

He seemed to know and hesitated. "Or I can wait until after the battle..."

"Caliban, you may be able to talk. You may even be able to will yourself to walk. But you cannot fight. Not now. Not soon. So you can stay here, an invalid, and force us to protect you. Or you can take my advice and return to Netherfeld."

He was silent. Alda heard the waves in the distance, beating against the shore so far below.

Caliban again looked toward the cliffs, and his face softened. "He is a good man."

Alda followed his eyes. "I know."

"No, you do not. Not fully. He would die for you, Alda. He would die for any one of us." He took her hand pleadingly. "Ensure that he survives."

"I will."

"And, and will you tell them why I left? If I wait to take my leave — they won't let me have it. Tell them, please."

"Of course."

"Also tell them I will return. Soon."

Alda nodded. "As you did in Fairy Land."

Caliban smiled as he raised himself and balanced on shaking legs. "Yes, to strike a hobgoblin."

They shared a silent, knowing gaze.

"Stay but a moment —" Alda stood and quickly pulled a broken timber from the rubble and tested it with her weight before she handed it to the beautiful youth. "Now, go." She paused and added, "May your journey end with a lover's meeting."

"'Til we meet again."

Caliban turned abruptly and limped through the dilapidated courtyard and over the low wall, toward the moors and distant beach. As Alda watched him leave, her heart seemed ready to burst. She doubted she would ever see him again.

His wounds were worse than he knew, internal and unseen, and there was no magic powerful enough to heal a broken body.

If there was, her grandmother would have surely taught her to use it when she first became ill.

At least in Netherfeld, Caliban had a chance of survival. If not survival, then perhaps some kind of existence.

So with a sigh, Alda turned back toward Dreng and Sycorax, slowly approaching over the palazzo's rubble. She took several deep breaths as they grew near until her voice was calm when they reached her side.

"Caliban is left to find Miranda."

"Should I go after him?" Dreng's voice broke with concern.

Sycorax shook her head and looked sadly at Alda. "Why?"

Alda lied, "He knew she was in danger and could not wait another moment."

"Is that all? Are his injuries more severe than we thought?" Sycorax seemed to know that Alda was not honest.

So Alda only nodded.

Dreng looked from the distance where Caliban had disappeared below the rise of the hill and turned back to Sycorax. "Will our plan still work without him?"

Sycorax hesitated before she met his eyes. "It will work, it will still work, with only us."

Yes, Alda hoped that it would.

Chapter Thirteen: Horribly in Love

Dreng's thoughts were a net of worry since Caliban left. He stood alone on the clifftops with the miniature book, his hand shaking as he read and reread the spells' words in his mind. Again and again. And he finally looked out to sea, counting the whitecaps to clear his mind. Then he whispered the enchanted words in his internal voice, from memory.

Because he knew that when the time came, when he faced the witches that had destroyed his childhood dreams and left him alone and unloved, he might not have the book. But he would have his wits.

He was suddenly aware that Alda was at his side, likewise watching the sea. He glanced back toward the palace ruins, saw Sycorax pacing nervously, and returned his gaze to the ocean.

"Are you ready, Dreng?"

He only nodded. "What did Caliban say, before he left?"

"That you are a good man."

Dreng blushed. "I wish he had stayed. But love can make a man do strange things." He looked at her, but she remained unmoved.

Alda did not shift her gaze from the waves as she sighed, "Do you miss it?"

"No, I am done with her."

Alda's cheeks turned a sudden crimson. "I meant your ship. Your life on the ocean."

"Yes, sometimes, but..." He did not finish. He could not tell her of the horrors he had faced there, of the strength it had taken to overcome them. Of all he sacrificed to lead his crewmates, only to have them wrecked on the rocks below. She would not understand, so he held his tongue.

After a moment, Alda continued, "Before the flood, when we were in my cottage, you spoke of a name."

"Yes."

"What name?"

"Mine." He looked at her, set his jaw, and continued, "My father's ghost came to me and told me my name." He looked away, not wanting to see her reaction as he spun the signet ring on his finger.

Alda was silent for a moment as if waiting for him to speak. Finally, she asked, "What is your name?"

"What's in a name?"

She laughed unexpectedly. "You speak like Caliban."

"No, this is not jest. What does a name mean?"

She frowned. "It is us. Who we are. How others see us."

"Then I am Dreng." He tried to smile at her, but he sensed his expression was something else.

"So before you were called that, when you were called something else, you were *someone* else?"

"Yes." He wiped his hair from his eyes as he

continued, "In a lifetime, we all play many parts."

Alda had a faraway look, as if lost in a memory. "All the world's a stage."

"Yes." Dreng hesitated. "The boy I was before is dead." He took a deep breath. "I should be, too."

"What do you mean?"

"I might have died before, long ago, in the hold after Prince Hamlet's escape, if not for you. And if I could have left this toil all behind, I would." He paused and corrected, "*Sometimes* I think I would."

Alda stepped back as if hit by a sudden wind. "Why?"

"I have done things since, experienced things, too, that make me wonder if this world would be better off without me."

"I do not —" Alda stopped, and Dreng could see her eyes search for words. But she composed herself and changed her tone, "If the witches have their way, there may be no world left for any of us."

"Something must remain, surely." He spoke with more optimism than he felt.

Alda studied his face, and her brow furrowed. "They drain magic, Dreng. What is left without that? Only chaos, like Caliban said." She met his eyes. "And we are all that is between them and a dark and joyless world."

"You will die to stop them?"

"Yes." She did not hesitate. "And you?"

"Of course. A thousand times, if I could."

Alda's shoulders slumped slightly at his response.

"Alda, I —" He stopped abruptly and stooped to his knees at her feet. His eyes searched the rocky ground, looking for something lost. He pushed aside her skirt and lifted her foot, retrieving something from beneath it.

She stood, bewilderment crossing her face, until he finally stood and met her eyes again. "Alda, when I was a boy, before I went to sea with my father, my mother gave me a token. A pebble from the shore, the last place where I stood on dry land." He held out his palm and revealed a black, smooth stone. "She said that it was my homeland and that it contained the love and power and knowledge of the generations that came before me."

His voice shook as he continued, "I lost that stone the night the witches killed my father. I always thought it protected me, somehow, and that is how I lived when he did not. And now, *you* need that protection." He placed it into her hand, his fingers covering hers for too many heartbeats as the waves crashed in the distance.

"Alda, all is about to change. The world. Our lives. But if we can bear this, we can bear all."

She nervously smoothed her hair behind her ears and started to speak, but stopped.

His heart sank.

So he stammered, pleading, "I only — I simply — I

need you to know that from the moment I first saw you on *The Tempest*, from that, that moment — I only wish that I could have found you sooner, before — before all of this."

She remained silent. And in that moment, Dreng, who had forgotten so much over the years, somehow recalled Caliban's words: "Doubt thou, the stars are fire, doubt that the sun doth move, doubt truth to be a liar." He drew a deep breath. "But never doubt I love."

Alda took his hand but looked down. He could not read her face as his voice quivered, "Never doubt."

Her eyes finally met his, and his arms wrapped instinctively around her waist. Through their tears — tears of joy or something else — they kissed.

Despite their too-many separations, despite their dream-like embrace in Fairy Land, despite all that had come before, Dreng knew this was real. This was the kiss that mattered. And he felt that she knew it, too.

Finally, he took a deep breath, his forehead resting against hers, before he again looked into her eyes and waited for her to speak. To react. He hoped that she might say the words he wished to hear. Words from her and no one else, not now or ever again. But she only took in a deep, ragged breath, turned, and released it silently toward the sea.

A sudden thunderclap broke their reverie. Alda stepped away from him and held her whipping hair as she turned back toward the palace ruins. "I came here, Dreng, to tell you it is time. We must face the witches now. Together."

She walked slowly away.

He waited for her to reach the palace's crumbled perimeter before he dared glance at the secret held tight in his palm: Alda's half of the cauldron's bubble, which he had so deftly lifted from her sock when he took the stone from beneath her foot.

Chapter Fourteen: How to Curse

As Alda walked away from Dreng, something inside her wanted to scream. But was it joy? Terror? Dread? Some combination of strange emotions?

She felt fear, certainly. Hesitation. The witches were powerful, and they threatened to consume all that Alda knew. But that was not the root of her internal turmoil.

No, this was more. New. Startling. It was from Dreng's words. His tingling touch. Their kiss. This was something Alda could not understand. Something she could not articulate. Something that existed better as a guttural scream than as mere words.

Which was why Alda had remained mute. How could she tell him how she felt? How could she convey such, such... She couldn't. Her words were lost.

And now, as she approached Sycorax in the courtyard of the ruined palazzo, she glanced over her shoulder one more time at Dreng and the ocean, and her heart rose into her throat.

Yet again, she pressed it down.

Within seconds, Dreng was at her side. Sycorax turned toward them both, her eyes anxiously scanning the skies. "They told me we would meet again. In thunder, lightning, and in rain." As she spoke, droplets began to fall. "Call them now, Dreng. I am ready."

"We are ready," Alda added.

Dreng held the book tight in his palm and breathed the words to the "pricking thumb" spell: "Call all about me in the dark, and like the savage salt-sea shark, I beckon thee with my own blood until the charm is firm and good."

They all waited.

Alda listened. And as the wind whipped her hair and blood-stained dress, she a did not feel fear. Instead, she felt only disappointment.

This was not the ending she had wanted. As a child, she had imagined being an old spinster in her cottage — alone, yes, but reading and cooking and happy. No, not happy. Content. And safe.

Now, after so much had changed, she still wanted to be happy and content and safe in her cottage. But not alone.

She never asked to be ripped from her home, hurled into disconnected stories that wove through other times and faraway realms. Before all of this, she would have been happy to become the eccentric maid on the seventh island, a figure in a fairytale told by local children.

But here, now, she could not return to the life she once wanted. She was trapped in her own fate like some prisoner in a castle dungeon.

As was Sycorax. And Dreng.

Dreng.

After he spoke, once he completed the words of the

spell, nothing happened. Silence.

Silence, and then wind.

Alda was about to lose hope when Dreng reached into his boot and produced a dagger. He held it expertly in his hand and placed the blade gently against his thumb.

Blood trickled from his fingertip as he replaced the weapon.

Then, lightning. Alda saw it strike between clouds before she heard the thunder. Another flash and thunder clap, closer. And then the ground heaved. Alda stood firmly, her feet slipping and shifting while she somehow remained upright. The earth seemed to rattle, its surface vibrating until the dirt fell away into tiny fissures, revealing a glittering, red granite stone beneath.

The shaking intensified, and Alda moved closer to Dreng as the stones and broken timber of the surrounding ruins shifted and tumbled down the mountainside. Soon the three were atop a smooth hill, thrust into creation by the powers of the magical storm, its crimson-granite surface reflecting the flashing lights above.

Alda looked to Sycorax, her fist clenched tightly around the pearl of wisdom. To Dreng at her side, now reciting the spell's words again and again and again, his voice booming above the noise of the storm. He was calm. In contrast, Alda shook with fear, her jaw clenched tightly and painfully.

Dreng, still repeating the words, touched her elbow reassuringly, and she realized this was not bravery. It was experience. This was not his first battle. And she would not let it be his last.

As they waited for the witches to appear, Alda knew that even though the forces were equally numbered, the odds were against her party. Her magic, her skills, were novice. Untested. Not like the centuries of power wielded by the wayward sisters.

Alda knew there would be death.

And she could not live in a world without — she could not live if, if her comrades did not. She would do what she must to protect him, no, them.

Sycorax turned toward Dreng and Alda, interrupting her fear, the blonde hair of her borrowed body whipping like a golden flag. "No matter what, stand your ground. We cannot give them an inch. If we do not retreat, the day will be ours."

Alda suppressed her apprehension, nodded, and again looked to Dreng. Sensing her dread, he smiled, took her hand, and squeezed her fingers.

The touch gave her some stirrings of bravery, or at least resolve, and she took a breath. "Dreng, I —"

More thunder. Lightning. Rain. The witches appeared, hovering in rising mist. Their black cloaks fluttered upward in an unnatural breeze, their hair curled and crazed, their faces shadowed with beards and hatred.

Dreng stopped his chant, and Alda expected them to charge, to attack, but they only laughed. Not a cry of mirth, but a cackle. Like angry geese on the Grand River. The sound gave Alda a chill, reminding her that they were less than human.

Or more than mortal.

Alda wondered aloud, "Should we speak to th—" The word stuck in her throat as Sycorax clenched her fists, hissed the secret words to an ancient spell, and loosed a burst of energy that flashed from her slight form in a white-blue light that pulsated in heated intensity.

Dreng turned his head away from the light, and Alda briefly shielded her eyes with her forearm. When she opened them, she saw the witches cowering, stunned, unable to move against the power of Sycorax's beam.

This was Alda's time to act. Her moment. And, for that moment, she had hope. The witches were held at bay easier than she expected. Or was it a trick?

She looked to Dreng, and each had something like relief in their eyes. She took a breath and readied to fight beside him.

But it was not as Alda expected. Instead of facing the witches, instead of muttering the words to bring the trouble fire spell, Dreng took Alda's shaking hand, and dropped something small and round into her palm.

As he closed her fist around it, Alda tried to scream out, but her voice was lost.

Before Alda vanished, before the cauldron's bubble whisked her away, she heard Dreng say, "I love nothing in the world so well as you."

But Alda had no time to respond.

Chapter Fifteen: Die to Live

"She is safe!" Dreng's voice was lost in the fury of the witches' storm. For a flash, he imagined himself again on *The Tempest*, commanding his men in the moments before he was washed overboard.

But Sycorax saw. The beam of light withered from her fingers as she wiped Miranda's golden hair from her eyes and held the pearl of wisdom to her forehead like a jewel in a crown. This was a spell Dreng did not know. One that was not in a book. This was deep magic. Instinctual. Something he could not understand.

As her fingers changed colors, turning from burnt orange to rusty red, Dreng braced himself for some impact. A whirring sound filled his ears. Then a scream, not from human lungs but like an injured bird. Then a boom like a cannon. And another. A third.

Wind whirled past him as the witches somehow took to flight.

The ground quaked, and Dreng lost his footing. As he pushed himself to his feet, scanning the dark skies for the weird sisters, a sudden fire filled the heavens. It was not the trouble fire, not a snare. This was new but familiar.

Sycorax had loosed St. Elmo's fire, the same flames that took his father's life and gave him painful scars.

But, strangely, he felt relief. This would be enough.

This spell that could bring such awful fury would surely stop the witches.

He looked to Sycorax, slumped below the lights that emanated from her hands and head, their colors dancing in the clouds above. She was intent, focused, so he scanned the space between for the witches. Nothing. They were gone.

Had they vanished? He could not help but smile.

Yet Sycorax did not seem to share his joy. She turned sharply, her
eyes filled with a wrath that Dreng could not have imagined from the
woman he once thought he loved.

And as he watched her, helpless, she burned. The St. Elmo's fire did not consume her. She seemed unscathed. Instead, it surrounded her, leaping in tendrils like some terrible serpent, high into the thunderheads and deep into the granite earth, which erupted in a shrill chorus of whistles and moans.

And although he held the ragged book in his hand with the trouble fire spell, he did not read it. He knew the words, not in his mind but in his heart. "Come deadly flames to charm the air..." And as he spoke, an orb of fire rose at his feet and shot like a cannonball toward the witches. The trouble fire combined with the St. Elmo's blaze to create a raging wall, a column that burned into the sky and sucked the air from his lungs.

Again, Dreng thought this was the end, that they would be victorious. He felt his shoulders ease as his nostrils filled with the scent of burning pine.

But the battle was not yet decided. Sycorax erupted like the sun rising over a waveless ocean, her flames illuminating the mountaintop in fierce, red light.

In a heartbeat, the witches fell from the thundering heavens and hit the ground. Dreng hoped, wished they might lie still. But they rose again, the three holding hands as they formed an outward-facing circle, chanting and spinning until the red-green flames of the trouble fire leapt into the air in a funnel and dissipated.

All was eerily calm. Dreng felt like he was within a hurricane, winds and chaos all around but eerie silence in its center.

And then he looked to Sycorax, the flesh of Miranda's body gray and spent. Their eyes met for a too-brief moment, and Dreng wanted nothing more than to run to her side and support her as they faced the witches together.

Yet he could not move. He was frozen to the spot, either by fear or magic, as he had been so many years before aboard *The Tyger*.

For a flash, his mind returned to the ship. A helpless, terrified boy who cowered as disembodied voices sang a destructive chant in his memory. Voices. Four voices.

The three witches, and...

Sycorax? But the thought was unwelcome here, now. Out of joint. Out of time. Too late.

So he could only watch helplessly as Sycorax collapsed, her clothes falling heavy on her sunken form as a puff of white smoke erupted from her body.

She was gone.

And Dreng was alone with the witches.

All he had were his words. So he spoke, again and again, the enchanted words for the trouble fire. Sparks erupted around him, but no more flames.

The witches stopped spinning, and all was still. But not silent. The mountain squealed louder, its rock grinding beneath his feet, wailing hymn-like chords into the heavy air.

And then the weird sisters were ever stronger, their eyes aflame in the murky darkness. Rainless clouds obliterated the sky. Thunder rumbled from unseen lightning. And the flames in the witches' eyes spit forth into a ruby sphere that hovered malevolently before them.

Dreng expected it to surge toward him, like some horrible shot, but it simply hovered. Then, laughter.

"He is but a mouse."

"Where is my Gray-Malkin?"

"No, we are the cats, sister."

"He is prey."

"Let him pray."

"Too late for that."

"But not to toy."

"A new one."

"Should we take him?"

"A fourth for us?"

"No, take him all."

"In part."

"Parts."

"Apart."

"And keep him for a spell?"

"Or more?"

"Aye, keep him."

"No, take him."

"Take from him."

They spoke quickly, their words overlapping as if they knew the replies before they again spoke. And with each word, Dreng felt a loss. Like grief, but more tangible. Something leaving from his soul. Something torn from him. Joy. Hope. Courage. Love. All the world's invisible magic.

The witches were stealing his magic as they continued to speak, sucking it from him like a horrible whirlpool as the wicked orb before them grew. And he knew they would use it to spread their chaos. To harm Alda. Or worse.

But Dreng could not flee. He could not attack. He

could only stand, rooted helplessly to a single spot as the mountain's squeals escalated into a discordant harmony.

And then he heard a sound. Not music, not exactly. But something deep and reverberating. Something both magical and grounded. Something from below his feet.

The crimson, burning mountain sang, its hollow notes twisting into something like a tune.

And Dreng realized the witches were right, the prophecy was true. He would not leave this place, not alive.

He would die here. If by their hands, the witches would drain whatever powers he might have like some leech gorging on blood. They would use him and leave him to rot.

Or...

He could not stop death. But he could at least meet it smiling.

As the witches chortled, he bent toward the ground. His fingers touched Caliban's dagger, its blade too cold within his boot. Before the witches could finish him, he held the weapon in his fist and steered its blade with all his strength into his chest, into the scar they had given him so many years before.

And as he fell to the ground, he felt a rush leave his body. Magic? Life? Certainly something seeped out of him, something warm and wet. Perhaps only blood.

Dreng tried to lift his head, but its weight was too much. His breath shallow. A pain in his chest that only increased as he gasped like a fish on the deck.

He felt like he was drowning. Drowning on dry land, so far from the sea. And as he floundered and fought for air, the witches stood in a circle above him, their red eyes gazing down like the fires of stars.

At least, he thought, *Alda was safe.*

Chapter Sixteen: Sorceries Terrible

Alda found herself in Netherfeld, surrounded by nothing. In her palm was the cauldron's bubble, its two halves fused in a line of bright blue. She was alone. In a void. Devoid.

Why did the cauldron's bubble bring her here, of all places? This was not where she needed to be. It was not where she wanted to be.

She had to get back, and quickly. Dreng should not have done this. He should not have sent her away against her will. It was reckless.

And where did he get a cauldron's bubble?

Alda felt in her sock. Her half was gone. He must have taken it and joined her part with his.

How?

When?

Of course, atop the cliffs. The black pebble was a rouse. He had stolen the bubble when he reached near her foot. And the brief, electric shock she felt when his fingers touched her ankle was distraction enough for her to not notice the half-bubble's absence.

And now, he was in danger. She must help him. And Sycorax. Because despite everything — they needed her now. She could not abandon them, not leave them to battle the witches alone.

But Alda's hands were shaking with more than fear. Her palms were smeared with sweat. As she tried to close her fist around the cauldron's bubble, it fell to her feet and was lost beneath the folds of her stained skirt.

She bent over, searching, feeling, groping aimlessly in the darkness for her one shining piece of hope.

And after too many seconds of fruitless searching, her hope likewise faded as she fell to her knees, her breath coming in shallow pants as the vast nothing around her felt all too claustrophobic.

She let her head drop back, her face searching what should be the heavens, as she wailed simply, "Where?"

"Here." The word was both calm and calming.

Her grandmother. Alda stood, her mouth agape as she stared at the shadowy, ghostly form before her.

"Gramma? Where have you been? I've looked for you."

"And I am found."

"But now I'm lost!" Alda's voice rose in pitch until her voice broke on the final word.

"No, now you see."

"See what?"

"The truth."

"Yes, the truth." For a moment, Alda forgot about Dreng and Sycorax and the witches as other memories boiled to the surface. She remembered the encounter with her grandmother's ghost in the cottage, and her tone became bitter, the words souring in her mouth. "That Phillida was my mother. That you knew she was in Fairy Land and never told me she was alive."

"She was lost, too, and I could only save one. I chose to save you."

"You mean *control* me."

The shadow of the old woman laughed. "No, child. There is power in our family. Your mother, if taken by the witches, could become a weapon. She was safe with the fairies."

Alda spat, "She was a prisoner."

"We were safe while she was in Fairy Land."

"*We*?"

"Yes, the world." Her grandmother paused and added, "She knew this. And now you know, too."

"Why didn't you tell me before? In the beginning?"

"I told you that you had to discover it in time."

"But you left me!" Alda felt petty for harboring anger at someone who had died, but she still hurt. Deeply.

"I had to leave so you could find the way."

"But the witches — they said a witch cannot die."

"When I died, you became my heir. More of my magic became yours."

"You — you *chose* to die?"

"It was my time."

"No, no." Alda felt a thick knot in her throat. "How?"

"A spell."

"But you never asked. You never asked me what I wanted!"

"You were too young."

"I am just as young now!"

"No, you have lived a lifetime since."

Alda took a deep breath and exhaled, uncertain how to respond. After a moment, her grandmother continued, "You have the legacy of my magic, Alda. A part of the ancient, extinct magic that the witches cannot control. That they cannot understand. You cannot let them take you. You must fight."

"How?"

"With my help."

"Help? Then help me find the cauldron's bubble, and I'll take you —"

"No, Alda." The old woman sighed. "I am a shade. A shadow. A soul without a form. I am weak. Easily defeated if I leave here." She paused, her eyes studying Alda's. "No, you must have faith."

"Faith?"

"In yourself." As her grandmother spoke, a streak of green light whirled above. A spirit. It came into form above the old woman, hovering some feet above Alda.

A Luna moth.

"Phillida?"

It faltered and fell several inches before it recovered. Alda noticed one of its wings was broken. A piece missing.

"You are hurt?" Alda's voice cracked. Its injury likely happened because of her, when the spirits helped her escape the witches.

"Do not spend your worries on me, child, because there is more at stake now than..." Her voice trailed off as she perched atop Gramma's shoulder.

Alda's eyes searched the visions of her ancestors. She wanted to say so much. To ask so many questions. But there was no time. Not now. And, perhaps, she would not like the answers. So instead of the past, she turned her thoughts to the future. "Help me defeat the witches."

"Alda," her grandmother's voice was soothing. Like a forgotten lullaby. "You doubt yourself. You think yourself weak and slow and incapable."

"That's not —"

"Listen, child. You think you are like the governess in that old novel. But you are truly a princess. No, an empress. The heir of Hecate. Stand alone. Command the magic. It will do as you bid."

"But *how*?"

Her grandmother's cold shade squeezed her hand as the moth alighted above, flashing green across Alda's face.

"Words. Release the words you hold inside like some

great deluge. The words will flow into magic. Flood them."

Alda remembered a poem that her grandmother often muttered late at night. "From out our bourne of time and place the flood may bear me far…"

But the final word was not spoken in Netherfeld.

Alda uttered "far" atop the crimson mountain, above the ruins of Prospero's palazzo on the enchanted island. In her hand was the cauldron's bubble, placed in her palm by her grandmother.

And before her was a scene of devastation.

The sky erupted in an unnatural storm. The ground reverberated with a strange music. Lights and rain and smoke and multicolored flames swirled like watercolors in a jar.

And the air smelled of an evergreen forest. No, a burning pine. Like the dead dryad.

Amid this turmoil were three hunched forms. The witches. Their faces illuminated from below with a pale, green light.

Alda braced herself to attack them, her fists shaking and her mind focused with the intensity she needed to — to what? To somehow channel the strength of her grandmother's ancient magic.

Alda shook her head, clearing her mind. Her attention felt like the tip of a needle, all thoughts narrowed to a single point, all else that did not matter pushed to the periphery and out of focus. She shifted the invisible beam of her thoughts to the witches.

Yet, her worries shifted. Where was Dreng? And Sycorax? Had the summoner abandoned them? And would Caliban return, with help from Miranda?

But Alda's heart sank when she saw him — Dreng — prostrate on the red earth, a strange glow emanating from his form. The witches above him. The culprits. She feared him dead but somehow knew he still breathed. She had to act quickly. To save him.

She wailed, the sound involuntary as her heart strained against her chest, and the witches saw her.

But, strangely and suddenly, Alda was not afraid. She smelled the familiar scent of rosemary as calm trickled from her fingertips to her toes. She moved mechanically as if remembering some old dance, her arms turning in ways that she did not understand as wind rushed between her fingers.

"He is dead." They laughed.

A lie. Alda did not believe the witches, their equivocation.

"Dead."

"And gone."

"No!" A flash. A rush of hot air. And a scream that Alda did not feel coming from her throat.

"You cannot save him!" The witches' words were a

taunt. A distraction.

Words.

As Alda gripped the black pebble in her hand, her body remembered her family's ancient powers, the sensation she had felt when she was trapped in the pit so many months ago. As a white-hot aura enveloped her form, she let loose the secrets of her soul. "I am little and young and inexperienced, but I am still fierce. And I am worthy. Worthy not only of my family's powers but of love. And I had that, all too briefly."

Her voice cracked, but she continued as her limbs tingled and glowed. "When I met him on the ship, I knew that — I knew there would be more to our lives. And that we belonged together. And I would never say it, never breathe it, hardly dare to even hope it, but I still *knew* in the depth of my being that our lives would be as one. No, they *will* be as one yet. We share some strange destiny, some future in which we are together. To the end. To the end. No, beyond that. To some happy epilogue."

Hail fell. Its icy orbs stung Alda's cheeks and hands.

The witches cowered as the flames from the trouble fire went out, replaced by something far more terrifying.

White lightning, leaving Alda's hands in blinding streaks and flashes. Reverberating thunder. And Alda's words, her agonized words, released in torrents of emotion, "Dreng cannot be dead. He never will die.

Because he is immortal. Not immortal to the rest of the world. Not some mythical god. But he is *mine*. As long as I live, as long as I breathe his name and whisper his life's story, he will live on."

Tears streamed down her cheeks as hot rain fell hard and strong from the heavens. "You cannot take him from me. And if what you tell me is true — if his earthly form is indeed dead, I know that is only his body. His soul lies elsewhere. Half in Heaven. Half intertwined with mine. You cannot tear him from me!"

Her face was drenched with tears and raindrops, red with anguish and hailstones. She closed her eyes, no longer caring about the witches or her imminent danger. Only Dreng. Only the words she could not say to him on the clifftop. "I love him. I love him. I love nothing so well as him! And I will save him yet! There is no power in all of nature or the heavens that will tear us apart."

Lights flashed behind her lids. Then a jolt of cold. She opened her eyes to darkness. Steam rose from the mountain. As the mist evaporated, Alda saw the silhouettes of the witches against the retreating lightning on the horizon.

No, not witches. Stones. They had turned to monoliths like those in the circle on the moor, three great boulders forming a triangle above Dreng's broken body.

Alda felt numb as she wiped her black hair from her

face and reached his side, taking his hand as she knelt. Blood seeped through a deep wound beneath his torn shirt, spilling onto the granite at his side. His hands were limp and fallen, unmoving. His breath shallow, fast, as Alda wiped his dripping hair from his forehead.

The strange calm was still upon her as Alda realized his lung was injured. Perhaps at home, in her cottage, she could do something to help. At least something to ease his pain. But here, here she could not.

Yet, there was hope. She had the cauldron's bubble, whole, intact. She could use it, take him to safety, and —

No. It would tear them apart, as it had before. And she could not leave him, not like this, not now.

So she turned, looking once again for Caliban or forSycorax, and saw a pile of clothes nearby, covered in a strange, white dust. Alda knew that the summoner, too, was gone.

Alone again. And helpless.

"Dreng, it worked. I —" She wiped a silent tear. "The trouble fire, you did it — I think the witches — they're gone!"

Dreng remained motionless. His features ashen and sunken. His lips, quivering, were blue.

All this, Alda realized, all of their toil, was for naught.

*   *   *

Dreng did not know exactly what happened next, after he thrust the dagger into his chest. No memory of falling or of pain. First, he had the sensation of light, of heat, but all turned to black behind his eyelids. Now, the ground was cold at his back, but he felt comforting warmth on his hand as he fell deeper and deeper into the enveloping darkness.

"Dreng, can you hear me?"

Alda's voice, calling him. He struggled against some oppressive, invisible weight, and opened his eyes.

"Alda." He forced the word out, willing his parched lips to move. His thoughts wanted to form more words, to whisper that he *knew* her, somehow, from the beginning. That they were to share a story. That their souls and their lives were intertwined, despite only meeting for fleeting moments.

But this was the end of their tale. The final act. No, the curtain.

He felt a wave of emotions. Not only sadness and fear, but disappointment. He had once imagined them living together, old and invalid, sharing a bed in some distant cottage as they dozed, listening through an open window to leaves rustle and birds sing and ocean waves crash. It was an impossible image, a fleeting hope of stability and warmth and all of the things that Dreng had never known.

A dream of home. Of love.

He tried again to speak, but the poetry of his soul was lost in a rattle. His eyes closed.

He sensed her crying, sobs wracking her body as she bent over him. He tried to open his eyes, to see her again, one last time, then to reach for her, to comfort her, but he could not will his worthless frame into motion.

Did she understand? Did she believe all that he had said before? Did she know all that he could not say now?

Did she feel how deeply he loved her?

With a rasping, final breath, he sighed, but no words escaped his lips.

Silence.

And he let the blanket of darkness fall over him, stifling his soul and comforting his shivering form.

His last thought came as a kind of instinct, a flash of consciousness: *If only he had more time.*

Chapter Seventeen: Dagger of the Mind

Alda felt Dreng's hand relax in hers. She leaned over his form, holding him, gasping, trying to coax him back into motion, into being. Into life. But her tears did not resuscitate him.

Yet she still held tight to his hand, as she had with Caliban. The black pebble from the clifftops pressed between their palms. She wiped Dreng's matted hair from his forehead, running her finger over the rough whiskers along his chin.

Her breath was shallow and fast as she held onto hope.

But his breath ceased.

Frantic, Alda whispered, "I am here, Dreng. I am here. We are safe now. Come back to me. Come back. I'm waiting. Please, please. Come back."

And then she felt for a pulse, wishing once more for his heartbeat against her skin. But his heart, too, was still.

He did not return to her.

Dreng was dead and gone. Past the bar, like in one of her grandmother's oft-quoted poems. His form cold and unmoving, his eyes closed to all.

Seconds passed. Minutes. Hours? She stayed by his side like one of the weeping women on a marble gravestone.

Finally, after what seemed an eternity, she

straightened his shirt over his wounds, covering the scar and puncture from which his life seeped. And then she placed his arms across his chest like a medieval grave on a stereopticon card: a knight in repose.

But as she squeezed his palm one final time, she felt a fragment of parchment. Prospero's tiny book of spells. Covered in Dreng's blood. She wiped it on her skirt and stood, her eyes searching the horizon.

Now, what should she do?

The moon shifted, and she saw a glint near Dreng's feet. A dagger. Alda held it too tightly as she studied its metal. It lacked a sheath. For a moment, she held it before her, staring at the blood on its blade. She could fall beside him, now. And sleep, or something like it. She shifted the weapon in her hands, feeling its weight.

Wait. The word reverberated in her mind. That was not the way.

She dropped the bloody dagger before her and, trembling, stumbled to the broken form of Sycorax.

Only clothes and dust. No body, no blood. Like the discarded costume of a travelling actor.

There was no one left, not here. Caliban had abandoned them. Ariel, too. Dreng. Sycorax. Alda's hands shook, so she twisted her fingers into a knot and pressed it against her abdomen. But the shaking spread up and into her heart until it escaped in a sob.

She could return to Netherfeld. Yes, to her mother and grandmother. To — to what? Live in darkness? In a land of spirits? No.

Dreng would not be there. Death would be a better escape. Because then she would be with him.

Again, the dagger seemed to call her. To beckon. So Alda squeezed her fingers into fists and focused on the present.

After some time, her breaths became more even. Her mind less clouded. She remembered how to deal with death, what she did when her grandmother passed.

So she scanned the rubble around her, looking for something to mark the place where her friends had fallen. A memorial. A gravestone. The palazzo's stones were strewn near the perimeter of the mountain, thrown aside by earthquakes and the fires' force. Yes, one such stone would do.

As Alda walked toward the rubble, the moon reached its zenith and shown through parting clouds onto the red granite at her feet. And Alda saw a shadow.

She was not alone.

Near the three witches' monoliths was a silhouette. No, a shade. A figure flickering between gray and black. Like her grandmother in Netherfeld, yet different.

Sycorax. In her true semblance of the girl once called Ophelia, not the borrowed body of Miranda.

Alda stared at the being, afraid to speak first. Finally, she approached it with the trepidation of meeting a wild beast.

And the shadow rushed toward her with an expression mixing both fear and joy.

"Alda, you are returned unharmed!" Sycorax smiled, the expression out of joint with her surroundings.

"Are you, are you hurt?" The word was not right, but Alda knew not what else to say.

"I am as I am. I have been like this before, and —" Sycorax's expression sharply changed as her brow furrowed. "The pearl of wisdom, it was not enough. The witches, they — But you, you are safe. Yes, *you* are saved. Because Dreng sent you away — And Dreng — Where is Dreng?"

Alda mournfully turned her head, and Sycorax followed her gaze. The shade flitted toward his body and bent over him, her ghostly fingers flickering across his face.

"The witches, they, they killed him, and I —" Alda could not finish as another thought entered her mind. "Did you know of his plan?"

Several heartbeats of silence. Then, simply, "Yes. He wanted to save you, Alda —"

"And you, you let him stand with only you against the witches?"

"I thought — the pearl of wisdom, its powers — I thought we would be victorious."

"You let the witches murder him!" The words shook with anger.

Sycorax's eyes landed on the dagger, and she looked sorrowfully at Alda as she whispered, "No, no. They did not do this. They would use magic. A curse. A spell. Not a blade." She paused and added, her voice unsteady, "*He* did this."

"He wouldn't."

"He saw himself cornered. Outnumbered. This, his escape." Sycorax straightened, her form hovering above Dreng's corpse. "He was more an antique Roman than one of our time."

"No, no, he would never, never leave me like that."

"He saved you. Saved us all. If the witches had taken him, if they had used him, his powers..." Her voice faded as she examined the three stony monoliths.

Alda swallowed, her throat suddenly too dry. "Will the witches return?"

Sycorax reached a shadowy arm toward the stones. "No. We are safe from them. Your magic is elemental, natural, of the earth. And the earth transformed them." Her expression changed, and she added, "You are like Medusa."

But Alda did not respond.

The summoner's eyes fell once more to the ground, to Dreng, and her voice took on a hollow, distant tone.

"My spell, my magic, my sacrifice... Alda, this was not meant to be."

"Yet... it is."

They stood in silence, Alda's bloodied, wet dress cold against her legs, her face expressionless and her mind vacillating between disbelief, anger, and helplessness.

Sycorax glanced again at Dreng and shook her head, her ashen features bent in sorrow. "We cannot leave him thus."

Alda nodded.

"We should mourn him. Honor him. Set him adrift on a raft. Like ancient sailors in their long boats." Again, Sycorax paused. "Return him to the sea."

"No, we cannot leave him alone, like, like that." Alda wiped a tear from her cheek as something between courage and regret stirred her heart. "He was yours in life. Let him be mine in death. Let me remember him. Alone."

Sycorax started to object, but the consonants stuck on her tongue. Finally, she tilted her head and relented, her shadowy shoulders falling, "As you like."

Silently, she vanished like rising fog, and Alda was the only living soul atop the crimson mountain.

Chapter Eighteen: Quintessence of Dust

Finally, the tears dried on Alda's cheeks as she stood atop the pale cliffs that fell into the sand below. The place where she last spoke alone with him, with —

But she knew that behind her, the green glow of the pyre's flames still flickered on the red mountaintop. Consuming the one thing she had wanted. And though she did not turn to watch it burn, and though she was too far to feel its heat, its flames were too close and too painful.

As the sun illuminated the sea before her, Alda sighed. She was alone, here. Sycorax had not yet returned. Caliban remained missing. But she had the cauldron's bubble secure in her sock, along with the miniature book.

And the signet ring that he had worn — worn until the last — spun in her fingers as she thought about her future.

A knot formed in Alda's throat, choking her. She coughed, but the sound came out as a laugh, a kind of giggle that was appropriate only for a lunatic. Alda tried to suppress it, but the more she did, the louder and more boisterous it became. It felt like someone else laughing, not her.

And suddenly a poem came to mind, one with a line she had spoken to her grandmother in Netherfeld, one that seemed too fitting now: "Such a tide as moving seems asleep… when that which drew… turns again home." No, she had lost those verses, those rhymes. Forgotten like a dream at dawn.

But she remembered a second poem, too well, one with words she could not fully comprehend until now.

"So we'll go no more a-roving, so late into the night." A pause. "Though the heart —" She inhaled, her ragged breath not sustaining her through the lines. She stared out at the sea, watching the white-topped waves, as she continued, "Though the heart be still as loving, and the moon be still as bright."

Her mind returned to the funeral fire that spit and crackled unheard in the distance behind her, the illumination that had once been Dreng, so she forced herself on, "For the sword outwears its sheath, and the soul —" She suppressed a sob. "The soul —"

Her voice stopped, and the final word echoed from the cliffs below.

"This is not the end."

Alda started at the voice and turned to see Sycorax returned, her shadowy form gray and transparent, but her blue eyes flashing with renewed energy.

Alda once more faced the sea, her tone dark. "He is burning."

Again, "This is *not* the end."

"It is."

"You will find happiness someday."

"I doubt I will." Alda's tone was bitter.

"Why?"

"Love is not for our world." Alda felt anger rise in her throat. "You and Hamlet. Caliban and Miranda. Phillida and Oberon. You and, and *him*. Me, and, and —" Alda wiped her flushed cheeks. "We are all the stuff of tragedy."

The two women stood in silent agreement for several heartbeats before Alda realized, "I could go to him." She spoke swiftly, excitedly, "I could take my cauldron's bubble and return to the time before he was killed. I could stop the witches and save him. And you." She looked at Sycorax, pleading, but the shade of the summoner lowered her eyes.

"You would risk the world for a single soul. The witches could capture you, Alda. They could steal your powers, become stronger. Invincible. They are dead *now*. If you go back into the past and interfere..." She was quiet for a moment, her brows furrowed. "I loved him, too, once, but the witches have been killed. Magic has been saved. The world is now protected. Do not jeopardize our victory."

Alda's heart raced and hands shook. Sycorax was right. She knew she was right, but still —

Finally, Alda steadied her voice and loosed accusatory words, "Why are you here, Sycorax? Why not go elsewhere? Anywhere? You are free. Like a spirit. Go as you will."

"I want to stay here." She paused. "With you."

Alda did not respond.

Sycorax continued, "Many years ago, my Hamlet told me to go to a nunnery. It was meant to be nonsense, yet there was sense behind it." She was silent for too long and finally added, "He must be dead now, too."

After a moment, she sighed and gently touched Alda's shoulder. "We have magic, you and I. We know something of its power, its spells. We can stay on this island, study our skills, record them, perhaps teach others. Begin something like a convent for women who are written out of their own stories. For outcasts like us." She took a shaky breath. "This is *my* island now, once again. Let's make it ours, my friend."

"I cannot — I am not your *friend*." Alda felt the lie in her words. Despite the hatred, the distrust, there was something between her and the summoner. Something akin to friendship, if not exactly such. "And I cannot stay here, not with, with —" Alda glanced at the flames atop the hill, and a piece inside her broke. She collapsed, sobbing, and Sycorax reached for her, but her shadowy form brought a chill like a winter wind.

Concern filled Sycorax's voice. "You are stronger than you know, Alda."

"But how do *you* know?"

"Because I am, too. Stay here, with me."

"I cannot."

"Why?"

Alda did not have an answer. But she knew this was not her place, not her time. She did not belong here. She belonged in Grand Ledge, on her island, surrounded by the memories of her grandmother. Of *him*.

The place seemed to call her.

"I must return to my cottage."

"What is there for you, now?"

"I don't know. Not yet. But I *will* know." Alda's voice cracked. "Or I won't. And I will die there, as I always imagined."

"You will learn to live in time."

"How?"

"Grief is like an ocean. You can sink, or swim, or learn to float on its surface. I float." The final word was too literal for a spectre.

"But I sink." Alda wiped hot tears from her neck.

"Then go." Sycorax's voice was firm, commanding. "But if you ever choose to return, I will be here."

So Alda forced herself up. All had seemed slow, since he died. Like walking underwater. And now that Alda finally moved, she wanted to do so quickly. She had to leave, to flee. So when her feet were steady, she faced her companion and opened her fist, revealing Dreng's signet ring in her palm.

"I was going to throw it into the sea," she explained. "So a piece of him could always be within the waves. But it was not his, not truly. It came from your Hamlet. So it should be yours, now." Alda set the golden circle on a rock at Sycorax's transparent feet.

To Alda's surprise, the shade stooped and placed it on her own shadowy finger. "You will find yourself again, but it will take time."

Alda bit her lip and wondered aloud, "Do you think we shall meet again?"

"We know not what this world holds. Or the next." Sycorax's lips curled into a forced smile, despite the sadness behind her eyes. "But I will find my way. As will you."

Alda nodded. "Farewell, Sycorax. Ophelia. Whoever you are."

She bowed her head. "Until we meet again, Alda, heir of Hecate."

As the summoner's shade spoke the final word, Alda stepped to the cliff's edge. She could use the cauldron's bubble on the island now, but Alda needed release. So she once again hurled herself from the dreadful summit and clasped her fingers around the orb.

As she fell hopelessly toward death, Alda vanished.

*   *   *

When the too-familiar sensation of movement and comforting warmth passed, Alda found herself alone. And she was safe. An autumn breeze rapped at the windows of her cottage, blowing sunset-hued leaves against the cracked and broken panes.

She should sleep. She was exhausted. The witches, his death, her fall. Each had taken something from her, and she had little left to give. But all was not well. She could not rest. There was still much to do.

Her cottage was ruinous. When she had left, swept away in the flood with him and transported into Netherfeld by the cauldron's bubble, it had been late summer. Now, when she returned, months had passed. So before the autumn sunrays vanished, she gathered candles and set to work.

Mud caked the walls above her knees. Mold grew on soft surfaces, and its black veins traced unclean curves up the yellow wallpaper and onto the ceiling. Furniture was strewn about as if thrown by a giant. Glass and ceramics broken. Yet somehow the stereoscope was safe above the fireplace, its warped cards faded but usable. At least she could yet escape in its images when her toil was complete.

This was not her only flood, not the first time waters had risen into the safety of her cottage. But it was the most severe.

Years earlier, Alda awoke to water pooled below the crib in which she slept. It was exciting, then. Something different and unexpected to pass the time. An adventure. And her grandmother had borne the burden, scrubbing and shining and moving their meager belongings into the center of the garden. "You are safe here, always. I will protect you on the island. And the rest is transitory. What we need, we will clean. Sunshine will make it like new," Gramma explained.

Alda wondered aloud, "How? It is only light."

Her grandmother smiled at the little girl. "No, it has powers. It can purify. And it can heal."

Now, after so many years, Alda worked alone in the moonlight, cleaning and scrubbing until her knees ached and knuckles bled.

As the sun rose the next morning, she stood in the garden and watched its beams creep through the swaying trees. She needed to heal.

In the new light, she took the cauldron's bubble from her sock and held it in the morning's glow.

It was empty, like a hollow soap bubble. Near weightless and practically imperceptible to the touch. It was empty. Without Dreng, she could not make another.

She was here, alone. And trapped.

She sighed, helpless. But not useless.

Three days passed. Three days removing all traces of the flood. She saved the sofa and armchair, some dresses, her favorite mixing bowls, her grandmother's handwritten recipe cards. The black velvet cloak that had once concealed the cauldron's bubble.

Some parts of her past survived. The rest did not matter.

No, nothing mattered. Because no matter how much she cleaned and concentrated and stood in the sunshine, he was still gone. Not only him, but all of the life she had known before.

For fleeting moments, Alda regretted leaving Sycorax. Yet each time, she reminded herself that there was something here for her. Waiting. She simply had to discover it. In time.

So as the sun eased down toward the trees at the end of the third day, she stood beneath the orange and red foliage and allowed herself to feel for the first time since her return to her world and her time.

She knew, logically, that Dreng would have died much sooner, if not for her. That he may have even died in the hold of the ship, a lonely boy lost at sea, if not for her sudden appearance. And then again, in Fairy Land. So she assured herself that she had helped him live for a little while, at least. Longer than otherwise. And even a small moment of time with him was better than none.

But it was not, not truly. And, ironically, Alda had always expected more time. She delayed speaking to him, telling him how she felt. She had imagined some future in which to breathe, to rest, to finally and simply converse. She needed more time. But that was impossible.

Still, she tried to find comfort in one of her grandmother's favorite poems. "'Tis better to have loved and lost than never to have loved at all." The quote was spoken only in her mind, yet she choked on a sob on the final word.

It was nonsense. Surely the poet who had written that was old. Or had never truly loved. Or held onto false hope.

Alda had no hope. Not even false hope. Only memories. So she returned to them, first flitting over the earlier events on Prospero's island, of how she rediscovered Dreng in the palazzo courtyard. Then again, when they met so serendipitously in Fairy Land. And then once more, before the palazzo crashed around them.

And their encounter on the clifftops, when he gave her the pebble. How she wanted so much more then. More than a kiss. How she wanted to tell him so, so much. Words. Words — words that she should have spoken. Words of love.

For a moment, she felt she was there again. The salty

air on her cheeks. Her hair wild in the wind. And in her
mind, she told him all. The words she unleashed at the
witches, and more. She told him of her dreams and fears
and how he fit into all of the hollow places of her existence.
How he would fill the void of her soul, if only — If only they
had more time together.

Her thoughts lingered there, not wanting to return to
the more recent pain.

But too quickly her memories enveloped her, not
letting go. The smell entrapped her first: a piney scent
atop the crimson mountain. Then the cold air of the storm.
And Dreng. His hair or skin or some other odor belonging
to a man. His hand on hers, for a brief flash. Then being
ripped from that. Passing through time and place to the
realm of nothing. Being helpless. Returning too late.

She should have stopped him from sending her
away, somehow. He should have told her of his plan.
They should have discussed it before the encounter,
together. They should have talked. Then, maybe...

Alda felt tears drip down her neck and returned to
the present. A beam of light broke through the trees and
caught her eye. She squinted and turned away, suddenly
too aware of where she was.

It was late evening. She was dizzy from so much
time lost in her thoughts. Lost.

Yet there was hope. If only...

Alda closed her fists and focused her mind, as she had before. Her thoughts narrowed, and, and, and... nothing. No powers. No magic. No more hope.

Dreng was not all that was dead and gone.

And she remembered the stone, the black pebble that he had given to her on the clifftop. Clenched tightly in her fist.

Her grandmother had told her of worry stones, meant to absorb sorrow or fear. If this was such, then it was surely full. So Alda turned back toward her cottage, near the front door where Dreng had once passed, and knelt on the flagstones. She dug her fingers into the dark soil near the worn threshold and deposited the pebble next to the foundation.

As she smoothed the loam over it, she felt like she had at her grandmother's burial. Although it was only a rock, she mourned for it. No, not for it. For him.

She stood suddenly as she realized that she could not stay here. Not another moment. So she turned sharply and crossed the footbridge to the Ledge Path and clambered up the washed-out trail until she reached the mural of the three animals. "When shall we three meet again?" The words inscribed below it were unexpectedly hurtful because Alda knew the answer: Never.

She turned from the mural, so beloved in her childhood, and trod the worn path toward the long bridge and its electric lights, gathering wilting flowers and wiry evergreens from the steep ledges as she passed.

Chapter Nineteen: Fortune Brings in Some

The cemetery was at once familiar and foreign. The summer leaves Alda remembered had turned yellow against the dark greens and blues of the pines. But even though the sun was only a sliver on the horizon, Alda easily found her way toward her grandmother's earthly resting place.

Yet as she approached its simple flagstone, she felt as though she was being watched. It was an unnerving sensation, something she had not experienced during her so many previous visits since her grandmother's passing the prior winter. Alda turned in place, feeling more curiosity than dread in this garden of death.

Then Alda saw a ghostly form beneath a blue spruce: half a man, only a torso and arms. Its incomplete silhouette obscured in shadows and movement. Hesitant, Alda approached, doing her best to always have at least one headstone between herself and the phantom.

Ten paces. Twenty. Thirty. Alda was nearly upon the figure when it — no, he — laughed.

And she realized this was not some ghost or ghoul. It was a man holding a worn spade, standing in an open grave. A gravedigger. His eyes smiled as he again looked at her, but his mouth and nose were covered by a dusty bandana. Despite this mask, Alda recognized him as the same man who had buried her grandmother amid laughter and inappropriately jolly songs.

"Here again, after so long?"

"I visit less frequently than I did before..." Alda paused and added, as if apologizing, "I have been away."

"I envy you an' wish my visits were as seldom." He grunted as he continued to dig. His accent was strange, distant. He was not from Michigan.

After several heartbeats of silence, Alda felt a wave of recognition and wondered aloud, "Have we met, elsewhere?"

"I know you, yes, and your handiwork." He paused long enough to wink at the bundle of foliage in Alda's hand, and she understood. He added slyly, "You wreathe my hands' work."

"Well, plants were important to Gramma." More silence. "I should go." She turned once again toward her destination, but the jovial man cleared his throat as he dug.

"What's past is prologue."

Alda again faced him. "What do you mean?"

"That's what this grave will say. Or what it will read. Rather, what those who read it will say to themselves. It's a kind of poetry, no?" The man stopped digging and met her eyes, his mouth and nose still covered.

"I suppose." Alda hesitated. "And ironic."

"Why?"

"To think that life is prologue. For what? For death?" Despite herself, she choked on something like a laugh.

"For *whatever* comes next." He leaned on the spade and wiped his brow. "Poetic irony. The end is the beginning."

"That's nonsense."

"Spoken like one who knows sense. Or one who has lost it."

Alda shook her head and said, more seriously than she intended, "I doubt I ever had it. Not enough sense, at least. Or good."

"Bad sense."

She nodded.

"And now?"

"I have even less."

The man cleared his throat. "In what sense?"

Alda again suppressed a laugh, amused. "In every sense."

"But you can still smell and see and hear and taste. You have all five."

"You forgot feeling," Alda corrected.

"You may have lost that. It is easily deposited here, with the senseless."

Alda started to understand his word game, his equivocation. "Death is senseless."

The man nodded, his gaze fixed with hers. "Some times." There was an unusual pause between his words.

"No, always. Death is always senseless. Useless. For naught." An image of Dreng, unspoken words trembling on his lips, flashed into her mind. "It is deaf and mute and tasteless." Tears formed in her eyes. "But it reeks. And it touches, too much."

The man shifted and broke their gaze, his eyes turning to the empty grave in which he stood.

A sudden thought occurred to Alda, and her curiosity escaped her lips, "Have you ever buried someone whom you love?"

"I do not bury anyone."

"Well, have you ever dug a grave for anyone close to you?"

"The graves I dig make them far."

"No, I mean, have you dug a grave for anyone that you love?"

"I do not dig graves for anyone, nor do I bury anyone. Only any *body*." He chuckled on the final word.

Alda's frustration darkened her tone. "You know what I mean."

"My knowledge is mean," the man snorted.

"No, I, I was serious, and you —" Alda faltered. She should not have asked. The question was too personal. It was rude to prod a stranger thus. "I'm sorry. I —"

He held up a hand, stopping her. "Without my wit, I am nothing. All is jest, here. Laughter is what separates the living from the dead."

"And dirt. And decay." Alda sighed. "And time."

"Time is all they have now. And it is what we lack, what we are missing." He motioned to the surrounding graves. "But they all stood here, at one time or another, and looked at these stony faces as we look upon them now."

Alda wiped a tear from her cheek, and the man's tone changed to something softer as he continued, "Look there, at that red granite monument." He nodded toward a waist-height gravestone, its top arched and carved with two clasped hands. Alda walked closer to it, and the gravedigger prodded, "Read it."

The words were covered in moss, so Alda wiped it away as she squinted in the dim light and read, "Stranger pause as you pass by. As you are now, so once was I. As I am now, soon you shall be. So welcome death, and follow me."

She stood upright and rubbed her back as she once again faced the gravedigger. "It calls me to death. I have half a heart to follow."

"No, no." He shifted the spade in his hands. "It is a reminder. All here were once alive. In a different time. Some, in a different place. If we had lived at any other moment, we might have known them." His voice lowered with a serious gravity. "Our paths might have crossed."

"Yes, but they are dead. Now." And as Alda spoke the final word, she felt too keenly the absence of her cauldron's bubble. "Now is all that matters because now is where we are. Where I am."

The gravedigger snorted, "But it is not where you *may* be." He finally lowered his handkerchief, and his too familiar sneer curled into a toothy grin.

"Caliban?"

His face was lean and worn with age, lines etched above his cheekbones and at the corners of his mouth.

Alda stammered before she blurted, "How did you — Why are you here?"

"You told me to find you in the cemetery, witch."

"I did not."

"You will. Later."

"Why?"

He flashed his sarcastic smile, "To tell you what to do."

"You know I do not trust you, so I might not listen."

"But you will listen to *him*." Caliban held out his palm to reveal another cauldron's bubble, shining and purple in the twilight. "As you are now, so once was I."

Alda reached for the orb, but hesitated. "How did you get this?"

"I made it." He lowered his voice. "It can transport two people, together."

Alda looked at him questioningly. "How?"

"That is something you will learn in time." He awkwardly cleared his throat and continued, "But the bubble's power is nearly used up. One trip more, or two. I needed it, before I could give it to you, you see, for Miranda, and, and — that is a story for another day."

He sighed and changed to a more somber tone, "Dreng was not always Dreng. There was once a time when he was called Thomas Chatterton —"

"Is that his name?"

Caliban nodded. "His birth name."

Alda lowered her eyes. "He never told me his true name."

"When you knew him, he was someone else. He was Dreng. But before all of this, before the island and Sycorax and you and me and Miranda, he was a boy on a ship. And he still is, or was. Not now, but then."

Caliban again offered the bubble, and this time, Alda cupped it in her shaking palm.

"Then I must go." She set her jaw resolutely, feeling equal parts ecstasy and trepidation, as she thrust her flowers into Caliban's hand. "Take these. As thanks."

"But these flowers are for the dead."

"You will be, someday." But Alda realized she had another question, "Did you find Miranda?"

"Time will tell."

Alda understood. "But you cannot."

The gravedigger shook his head, entertained by her frustration.

Alda lowered her voice as she considered, "Yet you said that I told you to come here."

Caliban nodded and grinned, his eyes laughing.

Alda continued, "Then I *will* meet you again."

He lowered his gaze and kicked dirt from the spade, but did not respond.

Alda blurted, "When?"

"Tomorrow or tomorrow or tomorrow or the last syllable of recorded time."

"Well, until then..." Alda embraced the strange man in the grave and awkwardly pulled away, wiping his dirt from her faded blue dress. "Caliban, try to be kind."

"As always, my dear witch." He made an extravagant bow, and Alda likewise bent toward the ground, a smile crossing her lips.

When Alda stood, Caliban was gone, spade and all. Vanished.

She felt a kind of nervous excitement, a sense of both butterflies in her stomach and a boulder crushing her shoulders as she gently ran her fingertips over the smooth surface of the cauldron's bubble.

She knew what she might do, but should she? *Could* she? After all, this cauldron's bubble was not hers. It would take her where she needed to go, not where she wanted to be. Where might it take her?

As she wondered, she sat, shaking, on the edge of the

grave, her feet dangling within its depths, and held her face in her hands and breathed until she felt something like calm.

When Alda finally raised her stinging eyes and sat upright on the grave's edge, she lost her orientation in the twilight. Her head spun, and she leaned awkwardly to try to regain equilibrium until she fell forward, head over heels, into the shallow pit.

The damp dirt clung to her hands and hair as she turned onto her back and looked up at the darkening sky, aware that death was inches away on all sides. She thought of the witches' words: *In the grave.* "The rest she'll know in the grave."

And Alda laughed, not only in her throat but in her spirit. Yes, this was her path. This is what she must do. The witches' strange words confirmed it. For a moment she steadied her breath as she examined the glimmering sphere of the cauldron's bubble in her fingertips. And Dreng's words echoed in her thoughts: "I only wish I could have found you sooner, before —"

So Alda clasped the purple orb in her fist and exhaled slowly as warmth washed over her. And she vanished.

A cold autumn breeze swept through the graveyard, rustling the dry leaves until they rattled.

*   *   *

"Take me with you!" The words hung on the dying boy's lips, their echo hovering in the damp air above him.

But the mysterious girl vanished. And the boy, bloodied and alone in the hold of *The Tempest*, lost his last, brief, shining hope of deliverance. And now, as he felt the warmth of his own blood pool under him on the warped planks, he knew he would prefer death to what might come.

The crewmen's feet thudded above and changed in pitch as they quickly descended the steep stairs. Two seconds, perhaps three, and they would be here, hovering above him. They would also find Ernesto's body, discover Prince Hamlet to be missing, and blame the survivor for both crimes.

Survivor. Dreng coughed. Not for long. And if he did live, somehow, if his body did not break from whatever punishment the crew saw fit, his spirit would surely die. He could not emerge from this ordeal whole, intact.

One second more, perhaps, before the crew found him. A breath. A heartbeat. But in this limbo, that second seemed too long, the wait an eternity. Death would be freeing. An escape.

He gripped the golden signet ring in his fist and awaited his fate.

Movement. Not the crewmen. Not Hamlet returned, nor Ernesto resurrected.

The scent of rosemary again filled the hold, and the girl appeared. No, a young woman. The same, but aged. Dressed in blue, her black hair cascading down her shoulders.

His eyes met hers, and though he could not speak, Dreng thought, *You are returned.*

She crouched at his side and brushed his damp hair from his forehead. "My name is Alda Reeding. And this time, I will not leave you."

His heart leapt as their fingers intertwined. And they vanished.

Chapter Twenty: What Dreams May Come

When Alda exhaled, she was once again within her cottage, the sky outside turning purple-blue in the approaching night. The bubble had returned her, here, now. This was where she needed to be.

And she was not alone.

The boy had lost consciousness, his limbs limp and heavy as she hoisted him onto the tapestried sofa.

The same sofa where Dreng had convalesced after their escape from Fairy Land.

But this time was not the same. That had been *her* experience, but not that of this boy. *She* remembered, but he would not.

And despite Sycorax's warning about returning to the past, Alda understood that — in her own lifeline, at least — the witches were yet gone, defeated. Sycorax was alone on her island. Caliban was elsewhere having his own adventure. All of that was real. And Alda remembered that it had happened. The knitting needle of her existence was still straight with a beginning and an end.

And Dreng was still dead.

This boy was not Dreng. This was Thomas. This was a different yarn. The old cut and discarded. This one tied anew.

This was a rebirth. A second chance. An opportunity to grow with him and, if fate was kind, grow old with him. And to love him, in a way. A different way.

Yet, now they had more time.

As Alda watched the boy sleep, she twisted her hands nervously and realized that the cauldron's bubble was clenched in her fist. Rather, its remains. It had shattered into tiny fragments, dust that fell to the floor like sand in an hourglass.

This had been her final trip, her final adventure.

And this boy did not know what Dreng had known. He could not read the spell to help her create another bubble. Thomas did not know magic.

Dreng's life before, what he had experienced with Sycorax and Caliban and the fairies and witches, and whatever happened before that, on his ship, all of that was now gone. Like a dream, once mistaken for reality, now not even a memory.

But although the past was gone, it was not entirely vanished.

She remembered. And from her memories, she could weave words. A story. She would tell him. She would tell him all that she knew.

She would give life to his imagination with words.

And she could show him, with the help of her stereopticon cards, which she stacked neatly on the table near him with trembling fingers. When he awoke, he could examine them. They could view the images of distant worlds together and live in their shared fantasy.

The boy could have two lives, one safe within her cottage, and one in the world of dreams and visions and the poetry of story.

That, Alda decided, should be enough. For now.

So she boiled water and gathered herbs to heal him. And as she prepared a tonic, she rooted her mind to the present, focusing on the details of this moment.

Now was all that mattered. And the future. Not the past.

*   *   *

The boy, who before he closed his eyes had been bleeding and dying, unloved and alone, opened his lids to a place of warmth and safety. *Home*. The word slipped into his mind, something foreign and unknown but so, so wanted. No, desired.

And there, across the small, strange, still room, was a girl. The girl from the beakhead. Alda. Aged from when he first beheld her, yet not significantly. Only some years his elder. But worn. And tired.

He watched her busy herself with something in a bowl, something that smelled of the scent he had remembered and then forgotten. *Rosemary.*

And though his side burned from his wound and his limbs were weak, he wanted to see her. No, help her. So he pushed himself upright, and his movement caught her attention.

"You're finally awake!" She dropped the bowl with a hollow thud on the table, rushed to his side, and knelt before him.

"How long have I —"

She took his hand. "The best part of four days."

The boy wiped his forehead, his fingers tingling. It felt like he had only blinked. "Where am I?"

Alda hesitated, her mouth opening and closing several times before she released a flood of words, "This is my cottage, on an island in the Grand River, near a town called Grand Ledge, that is in a state called Michigan..."

He barely listened as she explained the geography in some detail, her eyes beaming into his as her hands clasped his sweaty palm.

And when she was finally done, her eyes narrowed as she observed his confusion, so she added, "This is another time, centuries after you were on the ship."

He wiped his swimming head. Another time, in the future? Another place entirely? It was too much to comprehend.

Yet he was not afraid. He belonged here, somehow.

She seemed to sense his thoughts as she assured him, "You are safe, now. Dr —" Her tongue caught on a word, and she whispered, "Thomas."

"Thomas?"

"Your name is Thomas Chatterton."

He could not conceal his surprise. "You know my name? You know *me*?"

The girl nodded and removed one hand from his to wipe a tear. "Yes, yes! I know you."

"Who are you? An angel?"

She laughed. "No, of course not." She cleared her throat and confided, "I was once a witch."

"So you are magical?"

"I know a little magic."

"Teach me." He tried to sit but swooned, his head hitting the soft cushion behind him.

She sighed, "I cannot."

"Why?"

She stood and poured water from a flower-covered jug on the large table. He drank from a dainty, chipped cup, gulping its contents until not a drop remained.

Alda studied him, concern etching her features. "The magic is gone now." She paused a moment and added, "But while you convalesce, I will tell you a story, a tale of a life you might have lived."

Alda gave him a stack of images etched on

parchment. Not paintings, something more clear. Small and detailed, colored pictures of ruined buildings and exotic landscapes and flora and beasts the boy had never before imagined.

She explained, "You can look at these through my stereoscope..." She handed him a quaint device of wood and metal. "And see the world. From here. From safety."

The boy nodded, and they sat for several silent heartbeats as he tried to understand.

Finally, he cleared his throat and asked, "Alda?" She waited patiently for him to continue. "Are we two alone here, in this place?"

"We are not alone because we are together. We will never be alone again."

The boy saw his joy reflected in her eyes, and they fell into a comfortable silence.

Alda stood and returned to the mixing bowl, and Thomas weakly eased himself upright and studied the fantastical images on the cards. As he carefully turned them in his hands and squinted at them in the dim light, a miniature book fell to the floor at his feet. He struggled to bend over and reach its worn pages, his healing wound still painful and swollen, but he finally collapsed victoriously into the cushions with the tiny book in his hand.

As he turned its leaves, the dark, mysterious shapes within its pages bent and transformed into words that he understood. He read.

And finally, Alda reached his side with a spoonful of dark green liquid, and he drank obediently, his throat closing momentarily on its bitterness. After another swig of water, he murmured, more to himself, "This is a strange book."

She seemed not to notice what was in his hand. "What book?"

He held it into the fire's light and suddenly saw that it was streaked with blood. A shiver shot up his neck, and his words shook. "It, it speaks nonsense. Lists of fantastical objects and absurd phrases that I do not understand. Are they riddles?"

He glanced at Alda's face and saw the color drain from her cheeks. "Riddles? You can read them?"

"Yes, but I do not understand. What are these things? What is..." he turned several pages. "A cauldron's bubble?"

Alda stumbled pack, dropping the spoon from her shaking fingers. She looked at him as one would stare at a ghost, as he had most likely beheld her when he saw her standing on the beakhead. And she leaned against the wooden table to steady herself as one might grasp for support during rough seas.

The boy began to speak, but words caught in his throat as he struggled to comprehend his companion's emotions.

And then she smiled.

Elation spread across her face as if some light radiated from within. He had never before seen such an expression, such ecstasy. She was the most beautiful, radiant thing he could imagine. And he, somehow, had given her this happy reaction.

So he asked again, "What is a cauldron's bubble?"

"A cauldron's bubble? I will show you — soon enough — after you are recovered and healed. In the spring, when the wildflowers bloom."

Alda wiped an unexpected tear from her eye and sat next to him on the long chair. She gently took his hand and covered his fingers with hers. "I have seen a lifetime of strife, as have you. But I suspect you and I — we still have great adventures before us, Thomas."

He suddenly felt older than his years and, for the first time, truly safe as he whispered, "Together?"

She nodded.

"I would not wish any companion in the world but you." He smiled, and the expression felt strange on his face. Unfamiliar, but delightful.

Alda laughed as she stood, the sound sweet and high, and struck a match above the fireplace. She lit a wax taper as she returned to his side, and he watched its light dance in her eyes.

"Let's have a story now. About the lives we might have lived." Alda took a deep breath and held firm to his hand. "I've heard that the past is prologue, so that is where we'll begin..."

When shall we three meet againe?
In Thunder, Lightning, or in Raine?

When the Hurley-burley's done,
When the Battaile's lost, and wonne.

That will be ere the set of Sunne.

~William Shakespeare (1564-1616), *Macbeth*
Witches' Conversation, Act 1, Scene 1
First Folio, 1623

Alda and Dreng will appear again

with Caliban in a new, stand-alone novel

Caliban and the Void

to be released on

October 10, 2022

∞∞∞∞∞∞∞∞∞∞∞∞∞∞∞∞∞∞∞∞∞∞∞∞∞∞∞∞∞∞

The other two novels in this series,

Cauldron's Bubble

and

Double Double Toil,

are currently available from
your favorite bookseller.

A Note About Thomas Chatterton

Unlike other characters in my books, Thomas
Chatterton was a real person. My character who bears his
name was not based on the actual Thomas, but I chose this
appellation to pay tribute to a literary figure who deserves
to be remembered.

Thomas Chatterton was an eighteenth century English
poet born into poverty more than 100 years after
Shakespeare's death. Despite its brevity, Thomas' tragic life
story is worthy to stand alongside the Bard's plays. He spent
his childhood among the gothic spires and flying buttresses
of the St. Mary Redcliffe Church in Bristol, an orphan son of a
sexton who had left him a treasure trove of medieval
manuscripts.

These fantastical tales served as fuel for young Thomas'
imagination and later became inspiration for his feats of
forgery. You see, Thomas Chatterton was deemed too poor
to be a "real" poet. And his style did not fit with the
Enlightenment literature of his time. So he created a *nom de
plume* — rather a complete, fictional persona — named
Thomas Rowley, who wove epics about Bristol's romantic
past. Thomas successfully sold these widely praised
"Rowley" poems as legitimate manuscripts from the Middle
Ages, until he had the audacity to share his identity as the
true author with the popular novelist Horace Walpole, who
then decried the poems as immature and immaterial.

Thomas was devastated. He had dreamed of a life as a writer in London and had spent his savings to acquire lodgings, but with little reliable income from his writing and a black spot on his name, his options were dire. After weeks of living off scraps, too proud to accept handouts from friends and neighbors, Thomas drank poison and died alone in his cramped attic lodgings, the torn fragments of his poems strewn across the cold floor. He was seventeen years old.

And, like something in a tale by Shakespeare, his death was mistimed. Four days after Thomas' suicide, a would-be patron named Dr. Thomas Fry arrived at the poet's attic room, searching for the talented writer, only to find that his offer of employment came too late. But Dr. Fry diligently pieced together Thomas' poems and helped preserve them for future generations.

Now, Thomas Chatterton is widely regarded as the originator of English Romanticism, his poems having inspired the works of William Wordsworth, Lord Byron, Percy Shelley, John Keats, Dante Gabriel Rossetti, and scores of other literary innovators and dreamers.

So Thomas Chatterton's name appears in my book not because I directly based a character on him but because he lived out of joint with his world. Had Thomas been born in the time of his medieval epics, his narrative genius would have been lauded. Had he lived in the age of the later Romantics, his poems would have been appreciated. But he lived in the middle, not fitting into his own century. This is why he shares a name with Dreng: both were interlopers in their times, out of place. And both struggled to overcome their disjointed fates. Dreng's birth name is an homage to this young man who exited our world too soon but who still left an irrevocable mark.

Yet the name of Thomas Chatterton serves another purpose. It is a reminder to appreciate those who create, to raise up artists and dreamers and support them however and whenever possible. His name is intended to encourage readers to search for forgotten and undiscovered authors — silenced or marginalized voices — writers from the past and the present who continue to challenge and inspire but who might otherwise be overlooked.

Yes, Shakespeare is instrumental in all fiction. But others need to be heard as well. Listen.

About the Author

Amber Elby is the author of three fantasy novels based on Shakespeare's plays: *Cauldron's Bubble*, *Double Double Toil*, and *Trouble Fires Burn*. In the last millennium, she was born in Grand Ledge, Michigan but spent much of her childhood in the United Kingdom. When she was nine, she saw her first Shakespearean comedy, *Much Ado About Nothing*, in London. Many years later, she studied Creative Writing at Michigan State University's Honors College before earning her Master of Fine Arts degree in Screenwriting at the University of Texas at Austin. Amber enjoys watching Shakespearean performances — in person and on Zoom — with her husband and two daughters and divides her time between teaching at Austin Community College, traveling, and getting lost in imaginary worlds. She spent this year creating several virtual plays, hosting the *Jane Eyre* Readathon for Bring the Brontes Home, and also working on her upcoming novel to be released in 2022, *Caliban and the Void*.

Author's Note

In response to the *No Holds Bard* podcast's
#CauldronsBardflies book club question, "What is magic?"

Magic isn't simply spells and wands. Magic happens every day in the improbability of the mundane. Ever since I was a child, I have adored O. Henry's short stories because their twists and turns are all possible, so their magic is in their coincidence. We see this in our lives, too, but we often take it for granted. My favorite magical experience, one that I could never transpose into a work of fiction because it is so unbelievable, is the story of my husband: we were born two days apart in the same hospital and were released on the same day, but we spent our early childhood in separate cities. When we were ten, our families moved a few miles apart, so we met in fifth grade. In middle school, our schedules were generated by computers, and we were the only two people to have the exact same schedule in seventh grade; he was assigned seats next to me in math and English and was in my history group when we learned about Medieval England — when we reenacted fiefdoms, I was the Lady, and he was my Knight. We were friends but didn't date until high school, and he only agreed to go to the movies with me due to an epic miscommunication in which he thought we were going with a group. Somehow, all of these little twists pushed us together. That is magic. And, coincidentally, we moved across the country a month after our wedding for me to attend graduate school at the University of Texas in Austin, which is a mile from O. Henry's house.

The author would like to thank and acknowledge...

My publisher, Verdopolis Press, who continues to support and encourage me.

Malvern Books of Austin, Texas, which is still the best kind of "weird" and was once again kind enough to host my launch.

Mixtape Marketing for offering sound advice.

The #Bookbloggers on Twitter and elsewhere, who help connect readers with authors, with a special shout-out to Rosie Threakall for catching up outside of the blogosphere (aka in real life).

Literature Lady herself, Twitter thread extraordinaire @Literature_Lady, who talked with me about my books on her podcast.

Charlie Wallace and Adam Gobeski, who still put up with me after all these years and who, for some incomprehensible reason, allow me to occasionally join them on *Cinematic Respect*.

The #Bardflies and their fearless leaders, Kevin Condardo and Dan Beaulieu of the acclaimed podcast *No Holds Bard*. This community is the epitome of acceptance, open-mindedness, and appreciation of all things Shakespeare. I give you my hands.

Montgomery Sutton of the Rude Grooms for lending me his words.

The self-proclaimed "biggest fans" of my books: Alice Bloomer, who has seen more plays than anyone I know, and Liam Milner, who creates amazing fan art.

Susan Gebhard for being my source of enthusiasm and a companion for playground chats.

Andy Bates for carefully reading and catching my "mettle."

Jill Dickinson, who has been my rock(star) since Book One, and who is the most giving and selfless person I know. And Jill even gave me my beloved *Hamlet* pillow, which has quite literally had my back for Book Three.

Brandi Harrison of TypeJar Studio, who reworks my scribbles into beautiful cover art.

My mom, Pam, who is a fighter and the best Bubby to her granddaughters. Thank you.

Finally, the people behind Dreng and Alda: my husband, Tony, and our fierce little girls, Alix and Annie. You give voices to my characters and inspiration to me. Thank you, so very much.

And, of course, Bill the Bard, always and forever.

www.ingramcontent.com/pod-product-compliance
Lightning Source LLC
Chambersburg PA
CBHW022018170626
46808CB00001B/468

* 9 7 8 1 7 3 2 3 1 4 2 5 2 *